hannah's garden

Books by
MIDORI SNYDER

Soulstring

The Queens' Quarter Trilogy
New Moon
Sadar's Keep
Beldan's Fire

The Flight of Michael McBride

The Innamorati

Hannah's Garden

hannah's garden

MIDORI SNYDER

viking

VIKING
Published by the Penguin Group
Penguin Putnam Books for Young Readers,
345 Hudson Street, New York, New York 10014, U.S.A.
Penguin Books Ltd, 80 Strand, London WC2R 0RL, England
Penguin Books Australia Ltd, 250 Camberville Road, Camberwell, Victoria 3124, Australia
Penguin Books Canada Ltd, 10 Alcorn Avenue, Toronto, Ontario, Canada M4V 3B2
Penguin Books (N.Z.) Ltd, 182-190 Wairau Road, Auckland 10, New Zealand

Penguin Books Ltd, Registered Offices: Harmondsworth, Middlesex, England

Published in 2002 by Viking,
a division of Penguin Putnam Books for Young Readers.

1   3   5   7   9   10   8   6   4   2

Copyright © Midori Snyder, 2002

The characters and events to be found in these pages are fictitious. Any
resemblance to actual persons living or dead is purely coincidental.

LIBRARY OF CONGRESS CATALOGING-IN-PUBLICATION DATA
Snyder, Midori.
Hannah's garden / Midori Snyder.
p.   cm.
Summary: When Cassie's grandfather falls ill, she and her mother return
to his farm, where Cassie discovers a wonderful, terrible secret about her family.
ISBN 0-670-03577-7 (hardcover)
[1. Mothers and daughters—Fiction. 2. Violinists—Fiction. 3.Grandfathers—Fiction.
4. Sick—Fiction. 5. Magic—Fiction.] I. Title.
PZ7+   [Fic]—dc21   2002003724

Printed in U.S.A.
Set in Jansen, Gillsans, and Rezin
Book design by Teresa Kietlinski

for
Momi

⋆ chapter one ⋆

I DIDN'T HEAR THE PHONE when it rang that night. I was lying on the floor of my bedroom, eyes shut tight, headphones on, listening to Hilary Hahn's violin crashing through the Bach partitas at a killer pace. The sound was crisp as a green apple, fast and gleaming like quicksilver. I'll admit, I was more than a little envious. I had a recital in four days and it was going to be me up there playing that glorious music. I was prepared, of course. Three months ago I'd gotten the invitation from Rose Bay's Youth Symphony to perform as part of a big fund-raiser, and I'd practiced so much and so loudly that Anne and I had nearly gotten thrown out of our apartment. She'd bought me a big rubber mute for the bridge that muffled the sound. I despised it because it made me feel like I was playing underwater, but at least the neighbors had stopped grumbling when I practiced late into the night.

Still, in my heart, I knew there was something missing in my playing. Something I couldn't put into the music was driving the sound of Hahn's violin. I wondered what she thought about when she played. Maybe, as Martha, my violin teacher, had suggested, she didn't think at all; just let the music take her, speaking its poetry through her fingers on the violin and the long sweep of the bow.

Maybe, I thought, I was too intellectual, keeping the music out of my body like a thing apart, when I should have distilled it deep in my heart and blood. Lying on the floor, I ached, just wanting in the worst way to belong to that sound.

Even with my eyes closed, I knew the moment when my mother entered my bedroom. Anne has a scent of lavender that follows her like a faithful breeze. I guessed that somewhere out there beyond the partitas, beyond the headphones, she was talking to me, even though I couldn't hear her. I could have opened my eyes, but I didn't want to leave the music just then. Whatever it was, it could wait.

Anne kicked my foot once lightly and then hard a second time when I didn't respond. Sighing, I opened my eyes.

Most of the time, my mother is beautiful. Tall and willowy blonde, she has skin with the polish of ivory, and her wide-set eyes are a startling spring green. She had me when she was young, and even though I was now seventeen, Anne still managed to look like my older sister and not my mother. It was irritating sometimes, especially when boys gaped at her, tongue-tied and silly. But now, standing in my doorway, the phone clutched tightly in her hand, she looked a mess. Her dirty hair was secured by a number two pencil in a makeshift bun. She was pale, dark smudges under her eyes. She chewed her lower lip.

"What?" I asked, dragging the headphones off my ears.

"It's Poppie. He's in the hospital," she said softly.

"Is he all right?"

"They won't say for sure. Only that he was admitted last night and that they're still diagnosing the problem. They want me to come up there."

Anne slumped in the doorway. Her long legs folded up to her chest and she leaned her head wearily against the tops of her knees.

"What the hell am I going to do? This is the worst time for this to happen. I've got three papers all due next week. I can't go now," she said, her voice tight with panic.

"You have to go," I insisted. *Poppie in a hospital.* It was impossible to imagine him there.

"Damn it. This always happens," she snapped. "Just when *I'm* getting my life together, just when it matters to *me*, I have to throw it all in the air and go running to take care of him."

"But he's your father," I said, maybe more sharply than I should have.

Anne turned her green eyes on me. They were bright and hard. "He's your grandfather. Come with me."

I sat up fast, hearing the tinny echo of the partitas in the headphones as they slid away. "You know I can't. The recital's this weekend. Not to mention I've got a paper due in biology and a Spanish exam. Besides, what difference would it make if I did go? He doesn't know me anymore."

"Then go for me. Help me, Cassie," Anne said weak-

ly, pushing back the blonde bangs from her high forehead. "I can't do this alone." She looked at me, pale and
scared. I just crumpled.

That was our relationship in a teaspoon. *Help me,
Cassie. Do this for me.* I loved Anne and cared about her,
but I wondered sometimes if she had had me just to be
sure to have someone she could lean on. Last year, she
even bought me a Mother's Day card. It was kind of a
joke, but I didn't laugh very hard.

"I can't," I said desperately. "You know this recital
means a lot to me."

"Apparently more than your grandfather," Anne
sniffed.

"That's not fair. You're just trying to guilt me into it,"
I protested, my cheeks warm with an angry flush. Truth
was, her words hurt, but I wasn't going to let her know
that. I *loved* Poppie. But in the last three years I had seen
him twice, and both times he no longer cared or knew
who I was. He had practically flung me away from his
side as though I were a stranger. I pleaded with him, but
with his gaze firmly fixed on the forest, he ignored me. I
cried for weeks afterward, heartbroken and miserable
that the one man I had known all my life suddenly didn't
want to know me.

Anne stood abruptly. "Never mind. I'll deal with it.
God knows I always have."

She stormed out of my room and I heard her moving
through our apartment, banging chairs and slamming
doors, first the bathroom, then her bedroom. I stayed in

my room, out of her way, just listening to her anger. She was frustrated, but I also knew she was afraid. Going up to the farm, going to see Poppie, was not something she was very comfortable doing either. He had rejected me, but they had fought and his words to her were harsh. There was nothing she could do to please him, it seemed. I warred with myself to get up from the floor and say something comforting to her. But I knew if I did, I'd get suckered into going. Instead, I lay there, one arm over my eyes, and tried to wait it out.

"I'll be back later," she said coldly from my doorway.

"Okay," I murmured, my arm still shielding my eyes. *Don't look at her, or you're a goner,* I warned myself.

The windows rattled as she strode across the wooden floor and shut the front door hard. Alone, I sighed and slowly removed my arm from my face. The mournful strains of Bach's ciaccona whispered through the headphones and a familiar, invisible blanket of responsibility settled over me.

"Aw, hell," I swore up at the stars and moon painted on my ceiling. "Who are you kidding, Cassie?" I asked aloud.

I got up stiffly and shut off the boom box. Then I gazed around me in disgust.

My room was a disaster of cast-off clothes, some dirty, some clean, that lay jumbled together on the floor. The computer screen blinked with a half-finished English paper. Next to it were the crusty remains of a pepperoni pizza, two coffee cups, and a bunch of rumpled notes.

Books were everywhere, cracked open to reveal the information that was supposed to be going into a science paper. Sheet music had spilled off the stand and my violin and bow were resting on the unmade bed along with my CDs, some leftover bottles of nail polish, a plush pig pillow that oinked when you squeezed it, and most of the contents of my upturned backpack. Along my window ledge my plants at least looked healthy, leaves glossy and green, the hibiscus like a party girl with huge red blooms. No matter how busy I got, I never forgot about my plants. I rummaged through the laundry and found a clean T-shirt and jeans, changed out of my sweats, and headed for the bathroom.

Anne and I had made a pact two years ago when she went back to college and I started high school that we wouldn't bitch about keeping a clean house during Finals Week. I could see from the corner of my eye the stack of dishes in the kitchen sink, pizza boxes on the counters, and the trash bin on overflow. I peeked into Anne's room and it was almost a copy of mine. She had a thing for shoes, and there were about ten pairs scattered around the floor with the laundry. Embroidered bolsters were piled high on one end of her bed because that's where she liked to read, while all of her books occupied the other. On the night table next to the art deco lamp were a bag of chocolate chip cookies, leftovers in a white Chinese take-out box, and a cup of tea.

In the bathroom, I grimaced at my short, dark-haired reflection. My father had stamped me with olive skin, gray eyes, and a head of unruly black curls. It was just one of the things I hadn't quite forgiven him for doing— another was for being already married when he had met Anne. Typical Anne, she never told him about me. Just disappeared when she found out that she was pregnant and he was married with three kids of his own. When it came time to deliver, Anne headed home and I was born up at the farm, a pair of local midwives attending because Anne refused to go to the hospital. She hated hospitals, she said. Something about the smell.

I dragged a stiff brush through my curls, then tugged them brusquely into a rubber band as I thought over what I had to do. The first thing was to talk to Martha and explain why, after three months of preparation, I was going to miss my recital. I hoped she'd understand, since I didn't want to think about her being angry with me. Then on to Joe's house, to tell him that I wasn't going with him to prom, even though he'd spent a fortune on the tickets and the rented tux. *Well, it wasn't my idea to go in the first place*, I thought defensively as I brushed my teeth. I hated the whole high school scene anyway. But Anne had decided that after a life of us living like a pair of runaway bohemians, this was something I needed to experience, a chance to feel "normal," even though we both knew that would never happen in a million proms. I rinsed out my mouth, spit into the basin, and watched it swirl away down the drain. Tears were burning behind my eyes but I refused to cry.

I put my violin in its case and threw on my jacket. As

I headed for the door, I paused in front of Poppie's drawing that hung in the hall. It was my favorite of all his work. He had done it for me when I was a little girl and he still loved me. It was a pen-and-ink of wildflowers, and beneath the flowers he had drawn tiny weird creatures, their bodies made up of different bits of leaves, roots, and feathers. They grinned and squinted at the viewer, and one twiggy guy with an acorn cap had a finger stuck up his nose. Poppie and I had shared a sense of humor back then. I touched the glass, saddened to think of him away from the farm, ill and alone in some county hospital. It had to be far worse than the loneliness and hurt I felt missing him.

Tears burned beneath my eyelids again, so I slung my violin case over my shoulder and hurried out the door.

Anne and I lived on the second floor of an old brick duplex near the university. I bounded down the stairs and walked quickly down the street, my breath curdling in the moist spring air sharp with the smell of earth and last year's decaying leaves. It had rained earlier in the day and in the glow of streetlights the black trunks of the maple trees glistened.

It was late spring in Rose Bay, and the trees had already leafed out, shedding their seeds over the sidewalks and lawns. Front-yard gardens flourished with tulips, daffodils, and crocuses. The scent of honeysuckle and lilac drifted over the whole neighborhood

Up north, on Poppie's farm, the spring would have only just arrived. I pictured the forest that ringed the farmhouse, the gold tamaracks, white pines, scrub oaks, and solitary maples just now putting on their spring colors. Behind the farmhouse, the huge spiral of my greatgrandmother's perennial garden would be unfurling green and silver-tipped fronds from the mat of last year's dried leaves. A hardier strain of flowers would have braved the cold nights: the marsh marigolds opening their golden globes along the edge of the stream, the mayapples and trillium unfurling white flowers beneath the pine boughs. Alone in a clearing, an elegant pink lady's slipper would be waiting like Cinderella's lost shoe.

I walked with determination toward Martha's house, which was just on the other side of the university, in a much nicer neighborhood. Martha Fitzgerald had been a child prodigy, playing concerts when she was twelve. By sixteen she was winning international awards and was big on the concert circuit. Then something happened in her twenties; a nervous breakdown or a disastrous love affair, or maybe a bit of both. She returned to Rose Bay, met her husband Michael, an architect and wealthy enough to make her very comfortable, and she settled down to teach. Though their children had grown and gone to college, the Fitzgeralds still lived in their huge, old Tudor house, so different from Anne's and my ragtag collection of Goodwill specials. I loved being there. Every room had matching furniture, color-coordinated drapes, Persian rugs, and there was art on the walls, on the bookshelves, and over the mantel of their big fireplace. Martha even had one of Poppie's paintings hanging in the music room. That's how I knew she wasn't just well off, but really rich. Poppie's work only went to the serious collectors with big bucks.

And I think, initially, that's why she took me on, despite a crowded list of promising students. Someone told her I was the granddaughter of Daniel Brittman, "the famous but reclusive landscape artist," and she was curious. It's a good thing I turned out to be a decent musician, because I did little to satisfy her curiosity. Poppie had chosen to make his life a mystery to the outside world, and I was loyal to that stubborn trait. Besides, there was no way to explain Poppie to someone without making him sound, well, really weird.

We were always broke living on Anne's school loans and a small stipend that came from the farm, so I don't know how she managed to pay for my lessons. But I didn't ask. I decided it was fair payment for sticking with the violin despite all the cross-country moves she'd dragged us through, all the changes in teachers, and really bad rental instruments. When we moved to Rose Bay two years ago, I put my foot down. I wanted a decent instrument, a high school with an orchestra, and a good teacher. Three weeks later Anne maxed out a credit card buying my violin, called the music conservatory, and set up my first lesson with Martha.

I turned up Summit Avenue and could see the lilac bushes blooming beneath Martha's porch lights. A queasy feeling knotted up my stomach. Martha was a tough teacher but kind, demanding yet always ready to explain exactly what she wanted—and still a powerful musician. It always knocked me back a foot when she would play for me. If she even suspected you of slacking off for a moment, those black eyes nailed you, and the disapproval in her voice could crush rocks. *I'm not slacking off*, I reminded myself, but it did little to reassure me.

Heavy footsteps slapped the wet pavement behind me, and I turned around, startled by the noise. The sound stopped and I didn't see anyone. I scanned both sides of the street, searching the shadows of the trees in the lamplight. Bushes rustled as something unseen scuttled through, tiny branches snapping. There was a giggle and then a breeze ruffled the lilacs and the sound faded. I peered into the dark shadows, then upward at the long arch of the trees. A pair of eyes flickered green in the lamplight and an annoyed squirrel chucked at me. I turned away, feeling foolish, took three steps, and heard the slapping footsteps again.

I whirled around, spooked. A large rabbit bolted from beneath a hedge and galloped toward me. The creature was bold, moving quickly as its back feet thumped hard against the sidewalk, scattering water from the puddles. It stopped in front of me and reared back on its haunches, the better, it seemed, to view me.

"So, winter hare, a bit late for March madness, aren't you?" I asked.

It dropped to all fours and slapped a hind foot defiantly on the sidewalk, water glistening in its wet fur. Then it stood upright again and the shaggy-tipped ears reached straight into the sky. The mouth worked rapidly around two front teeth and its whiskers fanned forward as if to catch my scent.

"You're probably rabid," I insulted it.

The ears twitched and a gleam in its eyes dared me to approach.

"Shoo," I hissed, waving my arms. But the rabbit remained stock-still and completely unfazed. I glanced over my shoulder at Martha's porch and decided that if I ran fast enough, I could probably beat it if it was crazy enough to follow me. Maybe it really was rabid. So I turned and ran, aware I felt silly but also suddenly terrified, the violin case bumping against my thigh, expecting any second to be savaged on the ankle by an attack rabbit. Monty Python would have loved it. I huffed up the porch stairs to Martha's front door, rang the bell, and turned, prepared to do battle with a man-eating rabbit.

But it wasn't there. I was alone again on the street. "Cassiopeia Emma Brittman, you dip," I said using my full name to impress myself with the silliness of the moment. "Talk about feeling salty, letting Bugs Bunny push you around." I heard the door unlock and hustled to pull myself together again before I faced Martha.

"Cassie, what a nice surprise. " Martha's large frame filled the doorway, almost blocking the light from the hallway chandelier. She was a bulky woman, but for all her size, she carried herself like a queen and dressed like one in long, flowing linens, silk scarves, and Oriental brocaded jackets. Her black hair was piled on her head, secured with beaded hairpins and silver combs.

"Come in, dear," she said, and tugged me inside. "Are you all right? You look rather pale."

"I'm fine, thanks." I sure wasn't going to tell her about being scared by a rabbit.

Martha touched my violin case quizzically. "You're not worried about the recital, are you?"

"Not really," I answered. "But I do have a problem." I took a breath, then let it out quickly. "Something's come up and I'm not sure I can play in the recital."

I said it just like that. There was no other way. Anything else would have been like slowly ripping off a Band-Aid. Martha's pleasant smile froze on her face. A storm gathered in her dark eyes, and I swore I could see lightning.

"Come on, Cassie, you're too old for a case of nerves," she said.

"That's not it."

"Then what is?"

"My grandfather has been admitted to the hospital. I need to go up north and see him."

"Oh my dear, I'm sorry." The storm stalled and Martha's hand grasped mine. She drew me into the music room and I sat down on the butter-soft leather couch and stared up at Poppie's painting. It was a land-scape of the farm in winter. I could feel the cool snow, see the light shifting across the stubbled field, rays of fading sunlight catching on the dried stalks of wheat. "Is it serious?" Martha asked in a low voice.

"I don't know. They won't tell us over the phone," I answered.

Martha folded her hands in her lap and looked at me pensively. "Do you really have to go? Perhaps your mother can handle it herself if it turns out it's not so serious. It seems such a shame to have come this far and not show up for your performance. I would be glad to drive you up there myself after the recital, if you'd like."

It was a generous offer, but I had to refuse. I knew I couldn't let Anne go alone. And I knew there was no way to explain that to Martha without making Anne sound awful. "Thanks, but I really need to go now. I would never forgive myself if I wasn't there to help him when he needed it."

"Of course. You must do what you feel is right," Martha said, a little sadly. For a moment I feared she wouldn't want me as a student anymore. But she smiled and gently patted my shoulder. "You know, there is always next year. You were fortunate to get your solo as a junior. You can try again as a senior. And I am sure you will be even better. We will have to look for something new to challenge your talents."

"Thank you," I said gratefully. I stood to leave and for a moment we both gazed thoughtfully at Poppie's painting. Then I caught my breath as I noticed for the first time the small gray form of a winter hare bounding over the field. I leaned in to study it closer and an old song of Poppie's hummed in my head. He had called it "The Fiddling Hare," a silly song about the winter hare climbing down from the moon to learn to play the fiddle. When I was little, I'd tucked an old cigar box under my chin and leaped off the front porch, imagining myself in his place. Unfortunately for me, I wasn't so graceful. I landed in a yew shrub and cut my chin so badly on a branch that it took six stitches to close it. But once awakened, the urge to play never left me, and from that moment I drove Anne crazy with my pleading for a real violin.

"Wonderful, isn't it?" Martha murmured behind me. "Your grandfather is a great painter. It's almost magical. I swear it changes before your eyes, the light shifting, the little hare bounding over the field." She crossed her arms beneath her ample bosom and sighed. "I do hope he will be all right." Then she put an arm around me and led me to the door. "Take care and call me if you need anything. Anything at all. And give my best to your mother."

"I will, and thanks again," I said quickly, and slipped away.

On the porch once more, hearing the door lock behind me, I couldn't help it— I scanned the street, half expecting to see that wild rabbit again. Hoping, really, despite the fact that I had been scared of it. I wanted to believe it *was* the winter hare, one of my grandfather's creations come down to help me. But there was only a man carrying a plastic bag and walking his Doberman. I trotted down the stairs and fell in behind them, listening to the nervous click of the dog's nails on the concrete.

✦ chapter two ✦

"*DON'T BE MAD, JOE, PLEASE don't be mad*," I whispered as I rang the bell and then waited for someone in the Brennan household to answer. I could hear his little sisters shrieking, his mom shouting for Joe, followed by the furious drumming of feet. The door shuddered as someone slammed into it, screaming with laughter.

Then abruptly it flew open to reveal Joe's four-year-old sister, Stephanie, dressed only in her underpants and yellow socks. Her cheeks were flushed, her blue eyes sparkling.

"Hey, ditsy girl, what's going on?" I asked, tugging one of her braids lightly.

"Playin' shark." She snatched her tangled braid back and chewed the end of it.

Mariel, her older sister, suddenly careened around the corner and grabbed Stephanie by the shoulders. The two girls spurted away from the door like terrified minnows, chased by Joe growling fiercely, his long arms outstretched to snatch them.

I let myself in, set the violin case down by my feet, and stood in the brightly lit foyer of the Brennan house. It was big and open, with a large, comfortable living room whose plaid furniture could withstand being jumped on, survive peanut butter sandwiches and glasses of juice, and shelter feverish children propped in front of the TV with a bowl in case they got sick. The Brennans had six children, so the walls were crowded with wedding pictures, baby pictures, confirmation pictures, class pictures, and ever-expanding family portraits. There were country knickknacks everywhere, wreaths of grapevine with gingham ribbons on the doors, a carved wooden plaque that pleaded "Bless This Mess," and a wrought-iron key holder by the door on which the girls had hung little toys. The front hall closet was ajar, and it bulged with a variety of coats, big and little shoes, a hockey stick, a muddy soccer ball, a doll carriage, and Joe's mandolin case.

"Get in the bath, you two! I won't tell you again!" shouted Mrs. Brennan from the top of the staircase. I glanced up and waved at her. Baby Alice, naked and balanced on her hip, waved a pudgy hand back at me. Mrs. Brennan pushed wild strands of brown hair out of her face and smiled.

"Oh hi, Cassie. Say, tell Joe to get those two hooligans up here, would you? Or no bubble bath!"

"All right."

But I didn't have to say anything, for the girls magically reappeared, swirling and screaming around me, then scrambling in a thunder of footsteps as Joe chased them up the stairs. A moment later the quiet returned and Joe came downstairs, grinning.

He had a great smile, totally infectious. As anxious as

I was, I grinned back. I just couldn't help myself. There was a lot about Joe that made me grin like an idiot. It wasn't just looks, though Joe was well qualified in that department: tall, wide shoulders and a narrow waist, a head of thick brown curls, smooth skin, and cheeks that always looked flushed. It was really Joe's sense of humor that attracted me the first time I met him, in biology class. He was improvising a scene in which a frog incites rebellion among the other frogs not to go to their dissections without a fight. A sort of Kermit sings *Les Miz*. It sufficiently disrupted the class to postpone the dissection for the next day, by which time someone, we never found out who, had sneaked into the lab and liberated the creatures. That was my kind of guy, someone with heart as well as humor. Even Anne had found him charming. He found her interesting enough as a mother—Lord knows she was about as different from his as she could get—but much to my secret pleasure, he never turned into one of those gawky tongue-tied boys at the sight of her. It was me that he liked.

"Hey," he said, putting his hands around my waist and, after grabbing a quick glance over his shoulder to make sure we were alone, kissing me.

And that was the other thing I liked about Joe. His kiss. I'd met boys who tried to impress me with their coolness by slamming their mouths against mine, banging my teeth, their tongues digging down my throat in an imitation of raw passion. But Joe's mouth was soft and his lips folded gently over mine. We never banged our teeth or crashed noses, and except for the occasional raw onion hamburger lunches, his breath usually smelled sweet.

As we kissed, our bodies leaning close, Joe's hand slipped up under my shirt, brushing my bare skin to cup my breast. This was new, since about a month ago when we were making out in my room instead of studying. I can't say what moved me, whether it was Joe's kiss, the warm feel of his body beside me on the floor, or Vivaldi's *Spring* pouring out of the boom box. I felt his hands unbutton my shirt and just decided to go with it. Maybe it also helped that Joe knew his way around a bra hook and never tugged, wrenched, or snapped me in the back like some of the other dolts who had tried and failed.

But we were standing in his foyer, and his dad was probably in the den, because I could hear the news on the TV. I pulled away and brushed his hand out from under my shirt. He smiled, rolled his eyes, and shrugged.

"Can't blame a guy for trying."

"Yeah, but not here."

"My room?"

"Joe—"

"Yeah, yeah, I know that look. Shot down!" He put his hands around my waist and drew me close. "But later . . . "

"Joe, I need to talk to you about something," I said, pulling back from the distracting circle of his arms.

"Good or bad."

"Bad."

Dark curls fell over the furrowed brow and his face

became serious. "I'll get my coat." He turned to the stuffed closet and teased out his blue-and-gold letter jacket. The track medals clinked softly on the stitched varsity letter. He grabbed the black mandolin case in one hand and called upstairs.

"We're heading out to the session, Mom. Catch you later."

"Don't come back late, Joe. You've got school tomorrow," Mrs. Brennan answered amid sounds of splashing.

"Yeah, okay." Then he smiled at me. We both knew that a session meant coming home at two in the morning, at least. Joe would have to sneak in and try not to get caught. He wasn't too worried, though. His parents might complain, but they really liked it. They were heavily into the Irish heritage thing. Two of Joe's sisters did Irish dancing, and Mr. Brennan had a pretty nice tenor when he sang all those old songs. They'd all been to Ireland on some tour a couple years back and that's where Joe had first heard the mandolin, at a session in a pub. He liked the sound, so when they came back to the States, he bought a Gibson mandolin and a book and started teaching himself to play.

Even though I really didn't feel up to it, I had brought my violin, knowing that the least I could do after letting Joe down was go to the session. A local bar called the Dubliner cleared a space for folk musicians to come and play on Wednesday nights. It added ambience and brought in a lot of people willing to hang out, drink beer, and listen to free music in the middle of the week. It was really Joe's thing. He'd gotten good on the mandolin and talked me into joining him. He told me it would stretch my ear and keep me from being a music snob. I resisted at first, too busy with my own practicing, until Anne flat out trashed it and said I couldn't go. After that, nothing could have stopped me.

The first time I went with Joe to a session, it knocked me back. I'd been heavy into the partitas, trying to understand the written scores, trying to imagine myself a solo performer, and at the same time feeling burdened by the rigid discipline of Martha's scales, Kreuzer bow exercises, and a tyrannical metronome whose clocking beats I'd learned to despise. Suddenly, here was this unruly group of musicians playing tunes learned only by ear and heart, improvising ornaments and countermelodies as they went, pouring out this glorious rough-and-tumble music. It was as far from the front of an orchestra as I could get and I loved it instantly. It made me feel like Poppie's winter hare come down from the cold and solitary perfection of the moon to join in with the messy, noisy, hilarious earthly crowd.

Anne complained that it was dangerous. She wanted to know how the Brennans felt about their son playing in a bar late at night—which was pretty funny, because Anne got as nervous as a truant teen around such straight adults. But Joe convinced her that I would be safe with him and that his parents thought it was all right, provided his grades didn't slip. Then she argued it would ruin my playing, making me sloppy with the bow and wasting all the time and money invested in turning me into a decent classical musician. I countered by practicing scales longer and more diligently. And when Martha gave a limited approval, Anne backed down, even though I could see she still was pretty cranked about it. She let me go without too much bitching, and I chose to keep it on the down low to avoid any more arguments. But if I whistled a tune I'd heard, or played a bit of a jogging reel before settling down to practice, she'd glare at me, one brow arched in that Mother-know-it-all look that says *you're headed straight for ruin.*

We climbed into Joe's car, a beat-up pea-green Ford Fiesta. It smelled funky, probably from the discarded burger wrappers, muddy sweatshirt, shorts, and wet shoes all crammed in the back seat. His books were there, too, still in his backpack. Joe never studied much, but he was smart enough to fool most of his teachers into thinking he worked at it.

"You've *got* to clean out this car," I said, rolling down my window.

"After finals." He smirked, throwing the car into gear. "Isn't that the rule?"

"Not if I have to call the EPA. Baby, this site is toxic." I reached down and fished up a hard half-eaten burger and showed it to him. An empty soda can rattled back and forth beneath my feet.

"Hey, there's still some good eating there," he protested, shifting into second, then third, as he took the entrance ramp to the expressway a little too fast. I slid against the door.

"Gross," I said, and shoved the dried-up burger into a crumpled bag.

"So what's the bad news?" he asked after a moment's silence.

I stared out the window, watching the car headlights coming and going, wondering if there was a way that I could postpone saying anything. But there wasn't.

"I can't go to prom Saturday."

"What the hell!" he blurted. "You're kidding, right? I thought we were done with that argument. Cassie, you agreed to do this for me. Don't make me beg like some dork." Joe's foot dug into the gas pedal and the car sped up.

I clutched my seat nervously. "Poppie's in the hospital and Anne and I are going up there tomorrow." Joe swore and rolled his eyes. "I'm serious, he's really sick. We have to go."

"What about your recital?" He was watching me, his jaw tight with anger. Maybe he thought I was lying, trying to weasel out of going to the stupid prom. He pissed me off. I might blow him off, but never the violin.

"I'll miss it," I said coldly. "I've already talked to Martha."

In the headlights of the oncoming cars, his eyes were dark shadows. His body was rigid, his hands clutching the steering wheel as he shifted lanes to pass the slower cars.

"Slow down, damn it, or you're gonna get another ticket. You can't afford any more points," I snapped, a little scared.

Silently, he drove to the nearest exit ramp and got off the expressway. On a tree-lined street next to a little park somewhere on the south side, he pulled over and parked, jerking up the emergency brake with force. I couldn't see his face clearly in the dark, but I could feel the heat of his anger.

"It isn't fair, Cassie."

"Excuse me, this isn't about meeting your needs, Joe," I said acidly. "It's a stupid dance."

"It's not about the prom, Cassie. I'm not that damn selfish."

"Then what?"

"It's about you getting ripped off as usual. Sooner or later your mom's got to do some of this shit on her own. She whines and you jump."

"Poppie's ill," I said weakly.

"My grandmother had pneumonia all last winter. My mother went. I didn't go, my sisters didn't go, my dad didn't go. My mom handled it. Why can't yours? Just this once. Nobody knows better than me how hard you've worked for that recital, or what it means to you. I'm mad because you deserve this chance."

"I can always try next year. Martha said so."

"Yeah, and next year there will be a new crisis. And you'll be screwed again. Your mom's okay, but she's just too damn needy, Cassie. You have a right to say no to her and not have to feel guilty about it."

And that was another reason I loved Joe. He spoke up for me, made me question my own bad habit of always giving in. He let me see that I wasn't Anne's mother, that I was someone who had a right to find her own way. But this wasn't the time for that. Poppie needed me as much as Anne.

I bent my head and started to cry. Joe was right, but he didn't understand everything. My family wasn't like his family. We were fragile, thin threads held together by some mysterious force that sometimes felt like love and at other times fear. We had to pool our strengths in order to stay alive. Anne and I needed to be there for each other. It took two of us to take care of what was left of Poppie's waning reality. He was a kite, and without us holding on to him, he would drift away. Dumb as it was, I really did want to go to prom. I wanted to go to my recital. But there was no way I could say no to Anne or Poppie.

Joe held me close against his chest. The gearshift dug into my hip, but I didn't care. It felt good to cry.

"Hey, I'm sorry, Cassie." He rubbed my back. "Please don't cry. I'm being an asshole. You've got your hands full with those two. I should be helping you out, not yelling at you. I'm just sorry that I'm gonna miss seeing you play in that black, strapless number."

In spite of my tears I burst out laughing. Anne had bought that dress for me, thinking I'd be able to wear it both for prom and the recital. I had tried it on for Joe to see if I could play in it without feeling too awkward. The only way to get your fourth finger high enough in fifth and sixth position on the violin is to move your elbow deep under the neck of the instrument and, if you're female, sort of push your left breast out of the way with your elbow. So when I reached for the high notes, my arm shoved against my breast and popped it completely out of the silly dress. Joe had clapped wildly and shouted "Bravo" and "Encore."

"Look, Cassie, whatever you need," Joe said, and squeezed me tight.

"Do you have a Kleenex?" I sniffled.

"Hang on." He reached down, feeling beneath his seat, and brought up a wad of Taco Bell napkins that were reasonably clean. "Do you still want to go to the session? Or just chill somewhere?"

I blew my nose loudly into a napkin that smelled vaguely of green sauce. "Let's go to the session. It'll be good. Take my mind off things for a little while."

"Cool." Joe nodded and started the car. It coughed reluctantly until he revved it a few times, and then we peeled away from the curb in a haze of gray exhaust.

✦ ✦ ✦

It was one of those awesome Wednesday nights at the Dubliner when just about every musician in town decided to turn up for a chance to play and drink. We were greeted by the brisk sound of an Irish reel and edged our way through the crowd toward the circle of musicians planted in the back around a table cluttered with beer and whiskey glasses. There were at least eight fiddle players, their bows stabbing the air and skittering wildly over the strings in the fast-paced reel. A mandolin player, his pick hand a blur against the pretty flatback instrument, was shouting out the chords to a bouzouki player I'd never seen before. Two flute players leaned together like a pair of doves, the hollow sound floating easily over the scrape of strings. A bodhran player with a sweat-streaked forehead towered over a trio of guitarists. He held his drum up over their heads and added a throaty rhythm. Sitting among the fiddlers I saw my best friend, Genie. Her hair was lime green this week and it looked sharp against the dark fiddle tucked up tight under her chin. Her round face was lost in concentration as she worked to follow the intricate bowing. Next to her was a fiddler I'd never seen before, a redhead wearing a Moby T-shirt. Genie was leaning into him ever so slightly. Interested, no doubt, in more than just the music.

"Genie!" I shouted over the music, and waved.

She glanced up and spared me a hasty smile. Then she quickly lowered her gaze to the bridge of her fiddle, where the rosin puffed in little clouds from the fierce sawing of her bow. I took an empty seat just behind her while Joe went to buy us a couple of sodas. They never carded us at the Dubliner. They knew we were underage, but as long as we were there to play and didn't try to buy any booze, the bartenders left us alone. I took out my violin and bow, feeling the driving beat of the reel rising up from the floorboards through the soles of my feet. My pulse quickened as I set the violin beneath my chin, laid the bow across the strings, and waited. The reel was finishing its last measures when the redheaded fiddler whooped and segued without a pause into "The Silver Spear," a reel I had learned from Genie. My bow leaped to catch the first notes of the tune, and between one breath and another, I plunged into the music.

There's no better place to get lost than a good session. It's amazing to watch a group of near strangers lean into a shared center, all ears fixed on the music, all those different heartbeats joined into one by the demanding rhythms of the tunes. If the music's good, it's impossible to feel alone. *No wonder the winter hare left the solitary moon to join the party*, I thought, leaning back at the end of a long set of fast tunes, exhausted but happy. I plucked off the stray bow hairs that had snapped while I'd played. Joe shook out the cramps in his pick hand and complained good-naturedly about the speed of the fiddlers.

I wanted to talk to Genie, but she was busy flirting with the redheaded fiddler. It must have been the color that attracted her. Sitting together, they looked like an ad for a neon Christmas. I decided to introduce myself to the late-arriving fiddler who had moved his chair up close to mine as the reels progressed. I had been aware of him throughout the hour or so we'd been playing. He was good, really good—clear, commanding, always on top of the tune, and adding surprising little ornaments as he went along. I had managed to pick up a few of them and thought I should at least thank him.

"Hi, my name's Cassie," I said, turning to face him. "I don't think I've ever seen you in here before."

"First time," he answered with a slow smile. "Mostly I've been up north. But you sure look familiar. What'd you say your name was again?"

"Cassie Brittman."

"Brittman," he repeated. "That's an old name up north. Maybe I know your people?"

"I don't think so," I said quickly. "We're not from around here originally," I lied. Poppie's reputation up north was a mixed bag. Some of the locals thought he was pretty cool. Others thought he was a crazy old coot who attracted all the noise of unpleasant city folk trying to meet with him.

"Shame, that," the fiddler answered.

He started retuning his fiddle and, as casually as I could, I looked him over. He was an odd one all right. It was hard to guess his age. He had a shock of silvery gray hair, and his beard and mustache were streaked snow-white. But his eyes were a clear meadow green, and his exposed skin was smooth. I guessed he was tall from the length of his legs as he sat, his body primed over the fiddle while he drew the bow slowly over the strings. His clothing was rugged: red flannel shirt, suspenders, old jeans, and scuffed work boots. He carried the faint smell of wood smoke, earth, and pitch. But his hands were white, his fingers long and slender. Not a man who did manual labor, despite the farm clothes. Even his fiddle was unique. The scroll was carved with a woman's head, leaves curled into her hair, her mouth wide open as if she were singing.

The fiddler caught my glance and smiled. He took up his unusual fiddle and began to play a waltz. Its sad, sweet sound lifted slowly and caught the ear of the other musicians crowded at the table drinking beer. They stopped talking, and like ripples radiating out from the table, people throughout the bar gradually became silent, almost entranced, as the melancholy tune soared. The two bartenders, momentarily relieved of customers, leaned back against the counter, arms crossed over their chests as they listened.

I didn't know the tune, but I could have sworn the tune knew me. It called out to me, dug under my skin until I was sure I could have picked up my own violin and followed along without effort. It was a distant memory; there, just on the edge of my thoughts, almost out of reach, like trying to remember the taste of something sweet. Did it come from the north? Had Poppie hummed the tune while he worked at his easel and I played with my dolls in the studio? As I listened, drawn into the liquid sound, the notes splashed colors across the dingy walls of the bar until they were the deep green of the pine trees and the long grass. Gold, the color of sunlit wheat stacks and marsh marigolds, gilded the backs and shoulders of the listeners. The dark, murky corners of the ceiling brightened into the blue of an open sky and the long wooden bar was stained red as the clay on the stream banks, red as the cranberries and the painted clapboard walls of Poppie's farmhouse. I looked down at my violin resting on my lap and a wave of longing took me. I could smell the fields behind Poppie's house and the faint perfume of the garden. And I knew, as surely I knew my own name, that the fiddler played a tune about coming home.

I fought against the tears, and just when I thought I was losing the battle, the fiddler settled the last notes of the waltz as lightly as a bird on a bough. There was complete silence in the bar, and then, the spell broken, the room heaved a sigh, people clapped, nodded in appreciation, and reached for their drinks. The colors faded and the bar became just a bar once more. Noise happened, the scattering of talk, the clink of glasses, chairs being scraped along the floor. I wiped my eyes and looked up. Everything was ordinary again. I saw Joe thread his way through the crowd to talk to the red-headed fiddler, who was buying a couple of bags of chips. The gray-haired fiddler stood, stretched his legs, and then, instrument in hand, went to lean against the bar. In a matter of seconds, three shots of whiskey appeared in a neat row, all purchased by appreciative musicians. The fiddler grinned at the tiny glasses and upended every one, giving a little smack of his lips as he downed them.

"Unbelievable," Genie said next to me. "Totally unbelievable." Her hazel eyes were round like a Manx cat's, the lashes thick with mascara. She wore tangerine lipstick on her full mouth. "So what do you think?" she asked, pointing her chin toward the gray-haired fiddler. "Is he cool or what?"

"Or what," I said.

"Aw, don't be that way."

"Girl, he's old," I said.

"Are you sure?"

"For you, anyway."

"Yeah, but he can play. I could learn from him." Genie squeezed my arm.

"What about the redhead sitting next to you? Seems more your type."

"Hard to say. Either the guy's really stupid, or really shy. I couldn't get him to put two words together. Joe's looking pretty cute tonight. He's got that hair thing going for him."

I followed Genie's gaze to where Joe was standing, trying unsuccessfully to push his curls out of his face as he talked. He was flushed from the heat of the room and the effort of playing. Very kissable.

"Speaking of hair, what's up with the green?" I asked, tugging one of her dyed locks.

Genie smiled and ran her fingers through her hair. "I'm trying to talk my parents into letting me go this weekend up north to Ashland. There's a big music festival to raise money for the—ta-da—Green Party. There's going to be a lot of speakers—organic, no-strip-mining, preserve-our-woods type of folks. And a lot of these guys here tonight are going up there to provide the entertainment. Should be a good gig. Too bad you'll miss it."

"I might not," I said. "Poppie's in the hospital. Anne and I are going up there tomorrow. Ashland's not far from the farm. So maybe I'll see you there."

Her eyes widened. "You mean you're not going to prom with that hottie boyfriend of yours and you're not going to your recital? I can't believe it!"

"Aw, Genie, please," I groaned. "Don't make me explain again. I have enough people pissed off at me right now. Just be nice. Say you'll look out for me up there. Give me hope."

Genie shrugged her shoulders and opened her hands. "Okay, girlfriend. Whatever you need. Hey, wait a minute. If you're not using your boyfriend this weekend, do you think I could, you know, borrow him and maybe go to the prom? He's got that extra ticket, right?"

I looked at her closely, just to see if she was serious or not. Her round eyes were bright and unblinking. "Your hair doesn't match his tux."

"Isn't it black?"

"Lavender, with ruffles," I said dryly.

"Okay, I can take a hint. Leave the boyfriend alone." She grinned.

"That redhead keeps looking at you, Genie. Are you sure you don't want to give him another chance?"

We both glanced across the room and saw the red-head talking to Joe, but he kept turning and glancing back. He caught our stare and gave a short, very cool nod. He pulled nervously on his shirt and I noticed that when he talked his face grew deeply serious. Joe leaned down, the better to hear him. It seemed to take forever for him to get a thought out.

"I think he has a stutter," I said, guessing. "That's why he didn't talk."

"Oh, God, you think that's it?" Genie grabbed my arm again. "How cute is that?"

"Why don't you go over there and find out? And, while you're at it, ask Joe to come here. I'm beat. I'm gonna pack up and head on home."

"Sure." She rose to leave, then stopped. "Look, Cass," she said gently, "I know things aren't so good between you and your grandfather. Not like they used to be. But I remember my grandmother at the end of her life, mixing us all up with other people. In the end, it only mattered that she knew she was surrounded by people she loved, people who loved her, no matter whether they were ghosts from her past or us, standing there holding her hand. Talk to him, Cassie. Somewhere, somehow, he'll know it's you."

"Thanks," I answered, and really meant it.

She gave me her sweet smile, then turned, her bright eyes on the redhead.

It didn't take long to get ready to go. As I unscrewed the tension on my bow I felt my shoulders go slack with fatigue. It was late and I suddenly realized how uncertain I was about the trip up north, about Poppie. I couldn't get the fiddler's sad tune out of my head and my eyes itched from the smoke and the crying I had done earlier. All I wanted to do was go home and pull the covers over my head.

Joe held my hand as we left the bar. Outside, a flash of sheet lightning brightened the belly of some low-lying clouds, and I could smell the coming rain rising from the damp pavement. The Fiesta was parked about four blocks away. Joe glanced worriedly at the sky, and a gust of wind lifted the curls off his forehead.

"Look, why don't you wait here with the instruments. I'll go get the car and be right back," he said.

"You're such a good guy," I answered.

He kissed me lightly and headed down the street, ducking his head at a second flash of lightning.

I leaned against the wall and closed my eyes as the rumbling sound of thunder followed. The rumbling turned into a loud growl and I opened my eyes, confused, until I saw it was coming from a guy on a motorcycle, idling at the stoplight.

It was hard not to stare at him. Long, pale hair flowed over his shoulders and down his back. His features were sharply chiseled, exotic looking. The bike was big, but the rider was slender, his legs not much longer than mine as they straddled the seat, one booted foot barely resting against the street. His shoulders seemed too slight for the weight of his leather jacket. As soon as the light changed he nudged the bike toward me, and I realized with a start that he was staring back at me. I felt trapped in the beam of the headlight.

He pulled the bike right up to the curb and leaned forward to rev the engines. The jacket fell open, and above the slashed neckline of his T-shirt, I saw the dark blue-and-red tattoo, a vine of leaves and berries reaching up over his collarbone and around his neck. The wind turned, bringing the scent of gasoline and wet leaves.

"Hey, baby, wanna ride?" he crooned in a soft, husky voice.

I jerked back, the word "no" ready in my mouth. But for some reason I couldn't say it aloud. Tattoo spirals vibrated over the backs of his smooth, white hands.

"Come on. There's a place right here for you." He stroked the back of the leather seat. "I'll be good to you. Take you away from it all."

I should have been repulsed by such a blatant pickup, but the truth was I couldn't take my eyes off him. Up close, his face was beautiful. He brushed back a white lock of hair and the dark velvet eyes held mine. *Away from it all*, they promised. *It's easy*, I heard a voice whisper in my head. *Come on, don't be afraid.* I leaned forward, the idea, the boy suddenly irresistible. I could just climb on the motorcycle, press myself against his back, lay my head on that silky hair, and drive away from all my worries. He smiled at me, cool and sexy as the bad boy of every teen flick I'd ever seen.

"You're a musician, right? I know a few tunes," he said. He then pursed his lips and whistled. The tune was eerie, a little ribbon of red sounds that circled around my wrist like a bracelet and tugged at me to come closer. The leaves of his tattoo shivered. *It's easy, come on.* The strap of my violin case was heavy on my shoulder and the handle of Joe's mandolin case dug into my palm. I set them down on the street. Beneath long white lashes, his dark eyes glistened in the streetlights. He reached out an ivory hand, the spirals on his palm inviting, drawing me in.

I can do this, I thought breathlessly. *Yes, I should do this*, and reached out to take the offered hand, leaving the instruments behind me on the sidewalk.

"You forgot something." A gravelly voice cut through the whistled tune and stopped me.

I hesitated and the light wavered over the chiseled features. I wrenched my gaze away from the pale rider and turned to find the gray-haired fiddler at my side.

"What?" I asked, dazed. I shivered in a cold draft, my heart racing, my hand shaking. Lightning flashed and I heard the crack of thunder almost overhead.

"You forgot your rosin, Cassie Brittman," the fiddler said softly, and, taking my hand, pressed something into my palm.

I looked down at a heavy honey-gold cube. It was clean and clear, dark flecks like pine needles embedded in the dense amber. "It's not mine," I said, surprised by its warmth.

"Then take it as a gift," the fiddler answered. He turned to the pale man on the motorcycle. "Leave her alone."

The other scratched his chest, annoyed. The smooth white skin of his features hardened into ice. The dark eyes gleamed and he smiled at me. I felt a burst of fear and longing together.

"I'm gone, but only for a little while. I'll be back, girl, to teach you that tune." He revved the engines, popped the clutch, and nosed the bike into traffic. Across the back of his leather jacket the name BOG was painted, and below it was a white skull wearing a crown of withered leaves.

"Weird," I muttered, seeing the grinning skull lit up by the lightning, the teeth chattering in the thunder.

"There's your ride, Cassie," the fiddler said, handing me my violin case and then Joe's mandolin.

"Just in time," I breathed as big fat drops of rain began to spatter the street. Joe opened the car door and I dove in, for once not minding the funky smell at all. I started to roll down the window to say good-bye to the fiddler, and thank him. But he was already gone, a streak of gray turning the corner, and I had just enough time to roll the window back up before the rain began in earnest. Dimly, I wondered if the pale man on the motorcycle worried about getting wet. And somehow, I knew it didn't matter to him.

◆ chapter three ◆

I TOOK A LONG TIME saying good-bye to Joe. It was raining outside, so we pretty well steamed up the car windows. I whispered how sorry I was about prom a bunch of times in between long, damp smooches, and he told me that all I had to do was wear my new strapless dress and go out with him anywhere, even to the DQ, and he'd be happy. I agreed, kissed him one last time, then bolted out of the car through the rain and onto our porch. I waved before I went inside.

I tried to be quiet as I entered our apartment, but as soon as I set down my violin case, I knew I was alone. I glanced at my watch and saw it was almost two in the morning.

"Anne, you bad girl. You're grounded, young lady," I joked aloud, wondering where she'd gotten herself to this evening. I flung my damp coat on the couch with a sigh. I had hoped to tell her I was going with her, hoped to mend a few fences before going to bed. But I was too damn tired to wait up for her. Besides, I knew from experience what the late hour meant: a new boyfriend. I tried to remember if she'd introduced me to anyone lately. There was no one I could recall, except that film professor—a big, blond guy with an accent whom we'd run into at a coffee shop on campus. I'd dubbed him the Viking. But now, standing in the dark apartment, I dismissed the idea. He was too young for her. Besides, he was a professor, and there were rules about not dating students. Even though I knew she'd never taken a class from him, I didn't think she'd step into anything that could get messy. Finishing her degree meant too much to her.

As a rule, Anne had awful taste in men. Sometimes, she tried to conform to some creature she thought she ought to be. Those were the suburban boyfriends: a stockbroker once, a head of marketing another time, and in between them, a real estate agent. She told me she was doing it for me. So that I could live in a nice house with a real garden and have my college tuition paid for one day. I knew she also did it for herself, so I didn't feel too guilty. She got tired of managing things on her own. Some nights, I saw her sitting at our kitchen table, smoking the rare cigarette and looking over the pile of bills with a dazed expression.

Thankfully, those relationships never lasted. Anne just couldn't repress herself for very long. She'd wear a really short skirt to some corporate function, tell a naughty joke to the wrong crowd, alienate the suburban wives by being recklessly beautiful, and just get bored talking to people who didn't read and knew nothing about art. It didn't help that she had a daughter in tow. Frankly, I didn't like them either and refused to be anything but sullen, especially when they brought me CDs of the latest boy band, which I despised. They knew me about as well as they knew Anne.

After a breakup with a button-down boyfriend, Anne's pendulum would swing the other way but with the same lousy results. Worse, these guys never had money. A typical example was the chain-smoking painter who splashed turpentine everywhere and often set his shirts on fire. One night, when he was really drunk, he started to get way too friendly with me. Anne threatened him with his lighter and threw him out, along with his nasty paintings. A week later she discovered he had charged all of his long-distance calls to his agent on her phone.

When things went bad with a boyfriend, we moved, as if we needed to flee the bad luck these chumps brought us. We went to ordinary places—Cleveland, St. Louis—and then trendy places—Santa Fe and Atlanta. In every new apartment Anne would hang Poppie's picture before unpacking, as a way of making it up to me. Something like continuity, I guess.

To my surprise and relief, when we returned to Rose Bay, Anne had announced "no more boyfriends," at least not until she finished school and got her degree. She'd kept her word, and for the last year things had been pretty quiet in that department.

I sat on the couch in the dark and rubbed my eyes. I could still feel Joe's kiss on my lips, catch the scent of his skin on my hands. It was comforting. It was nice. How could I blame her for wanting the same sweetness? So maybe she had a new man. So what? Maybe things would work out this time. One could always hope.

I dragged myself into my bedroom, stripped off my jeans, and shoved everything off the bed. The window was open and a cool breeze danced across my face. I glanced outside as I closed it and there on the moonlit lawn was that rabbit again, looking wet and miserable. He reared back on his haunches and raised his front paws to me. I laughed. Poppie's winter hare, it seemed, was following me around. As I closed the window, he thumped his back feet and disappeared under a bush.

I couldn't sleep. I kept hearing the sound of an engine revving, going up and down the street. Some stupid college kid probably, frustrated because his date bounced him. I groaned and curled up into a ball. The sound got louder, almost insistent. I threw out a hand, groping for the boom box, punched the play button, grabbed the headphones from the floor, and put them on. Bach streamed into my ears, drowning it all out. Within moments, I was fast asleep.

I don't know when Anne got home, but she finally came into my room. She took my headphones off and ran her fingers through my hair.

"Anne, I'm sorry," I murmured into my pillow.

She didn't answer, but I thought I heard her humming. It was such a sad sound and, without effort, the fiddler's waltz came back to haunt the rest of my sleep.

✦ ✦ ✦

Sometime in the late morning I heard Anne get up,

shuffle into the bathroom, then return to bed. There was thump as some books got pushed to the floor. The sun was streaming into my window. I yawned widely, stretched, and got up.

Anne and I had another agreement. I put on the kettle. She made the coffee. Each one of us got an extra three minutes in bed. In the morning light, the kettle perched like a hen on the stove. I lit the gas burner and started to leave. A thought stopped me at the kitchen door and I backtracked. Lifting the kettle experimentally, I realized there was no water in it. "Caught you!" I said. I'd burned a few in the past, waking not to the scent of fresh-brewed coffee, but seared metal. I refilled the kettle, set it down on the nest of blue flame, and stumbled back to bed again.

I was still tired, but it was impossible to sleep. I lay there and thought about what I should take and what I was going to say to Anne. I thought about Poppie, about the last time I'd seen him, stoop-shouldered and grizzled-gray, wandering the edges of the forest shouting at the trees. A car backfired in the street and the Bog-boy with the motorcycle came to mind, too. I shivered and listened for the sound of the kettle.

It whistled shrilly and Anne swore in her bedroom. The bed creaked, another book fell with a thump, then her socks whispered across the wooden floors into the kitchen. The shrill whistle was replaced by the rasp of the coffee grinder. Then there was the gentle sound of water being poured and the glorious smell of coffee. I got up and went to the kitchen.

Anne had propped her elbow on the counter and, her face resting in her palm, was watching the coffee drip through the filter, first into her yellow cup, then over to my blue one. In my old Snoopy nightshirt and baggy socks, her hair in two loose braids, she looked about twelve years old—until she glanced up at me with a sad, troubled smile. Her eyes widened and the smile turned quizzical.

"What's with the hair? You let Genie do that to you?" she asked.

"What do you mean?" I asked, reaching up. It felt matted, like dreadlocks.

"Go have a look. It's pretty strange."

I walked into the bathroom, looked into the mirror over the sink, and shrieked. My hair was tangled with hundreds of little knots in a thorny crown around my head. Anne followed me to the bathroom with my coffee cup and stood in the hallway laughing.

"You look like one of Poppie's drawings! What possessed you to do such a goofy thing? I hope you didn't get any tattoos to go with those dreads."

"It wasn't me, I swear. I came home and crashed." But the knotted tangles argued that *somebody* had been busy. Stalks of grass, tiny snail shells, and dried leaves were all rolled into the snarls. It made no sense.

"I have no idea what happened," I said, grabbing my coffee cup from Anne, who continued to regard me with a skeptical stare. "But you should know, you came into my room."

"No, I didn't," Anne said. She blanched, her eyes growing dark. She reached out to touch my hair, then drew back.

I took a huge swig of coffee and instantly spat it out into the sink. It tasted thick and sour. White clots of milk floated along the rim.

"Yuck, the milk's gone sour."

"Impossible," Anne exclaimed. "I bought it yesterday!"

I thrust my cup under her nose and she grimaced before taking it. "Sorry," she apologized. "It must be that convenience store. Who knows how old the milk is before you buy it."

"Never mind," I grumbled.

"Listen, get that stuff out of your hair. It's a mess," she said, and turned on the shower.

"You don't like me as Mrs. Tiggywinkle?" I asked.

"No," she snapped. "You look ridiculous."

The shower was hot and steamy. Small lines of dirty water streamed over my shoulders and down the length of my body. I pulled the dry flower stalks, the snail shells and leaves out of my knotted hair. The shampoo suds around my ankles were tea-colored. I couldn't imagine what had happened. Someone had been in my room last night. Someone had hummed that tune and tricked out my hair. First the winter hare on my front lawn, then the man on the motorcycle. And now this. I should have been more worried, more scared. And yet something about it felt familiar. Déjà vu, almost.

"Anne, listen," I shouted as I washed my hair a second time. "I wanted to let you know that I'm coming with you."

"What?" she shouted back.

I finished rinsing the soapsuds out of my hair and turned off the water. "I said I'm coming with you. I talked to Martha and Joe last night and told them. It's all set. Except for school, but we can deal with that later."

"Oh, Cassie," she groaned from the other room.

I wrapped myself in a towel, walked into the kitchen, and found the Viking sitting at the table, a cup of black coffee in his hand. Anne was sitting next to him, her cheeks pink with embarrassment.

"You remember Gunnar, don't you, Cassie?" Anne asked in an airy voice.

"We met at the Comet Coffeehouse," he added, smiling.

"Sure," I said. *Oh, great, so you're the new boyfriend,* I thought. I clutched my towel a little tighter around my chest. Nothing like standing bare-assed in the kitchen with your mother's gorgeous boyfriend first thing in the morning. I blushed to my newly cleaned roots. "I gotta get some clothes on," I mumbled, and bolted.

I grabbed a clean Powerpuff Girls T-shirt and my jeans from last night. They stank of the bar, smoke, and someone else's spilled beer. I didn't care. I wasn't out to impress anyone. I tried to comb out my wet curls but just gave up because I knew I was stalling. *What was she thinking, picking up a professor?* I railed to my socks and tennies. *Why does she do this herself, to me? Guy's a flipping child.* I jerked the laces tight as my anger bloomed.

But walking into the kitchen a second time, I was struck by how cozy they looked and what a pretty pair they made sitting together. The Viking was clean-shaven, with dark blond hair that curled over the edges of the collar of a very expensive leather jacket. Everything about him seemed solid: the wide forehead, long nose, and squared chin. Even his hands on the table looked very capable. They were broad with tapered fingers and clean nails.

Anne held up a new carton of milk like a peace offering. "Gunnar brought some fresh milk."

"Thanks," I said, and sat down with them.

There was an awkward silence as I poured the milk into my coffee and, head down, stirred it, waiting for one of them to say something.

"Gunnar has offered to drive me up north, Cassie."

My head shot up. "Are you sure you want to do that?" I asked, eyebrows raised. Anne pursed her lips and looked away. She knew why I asked. Boyfriends didn't fare well up at the farm. The last guy was a carpenter, and our visit was cut short when Poppie lit out after him with a birch switch, shouting, "Bastard, get out," at the top of his lungs. Poppie was old, but he wasn't frail. Wasn't entirely crazy either. Anne's carpenter had dropped us off at home, taken our car to buy a few groceries, and never come back. Turned out he'd been setting up a deal with an art dealer in town. He stole two of

Poppie's paintings, sold them, and ditched. The paintings were never recovered, and Anne never really forgave herself.

"I would like to help Anne any way I can," Gunnar answered for her. He had a lilt to his voice, a singsong that at any other time I might have found charming. Now it annoyed me.

"Well, I'm coming, too," I said defiantly, and it was Anne's turn to look surprised.

"And your recital? The prom?"

I shrugged, stone-faced. "I took care of it."

"That's great. It's good that you can come, too," Gunnar said.

Jerk. The Viking had no idea what this trip had cost me. He made it seem like I was giving up a dentist appointment.

"I'm sure your mother and grandfather will really appreciate it. And it will give us a chance to spend some time together," he added.

I looked at his face, trying to see what hidden agenda was there. He was hard to read, the blue eyes cool and neutral, just checking me out. Anne wore a hopeful expression, but she knew better. I was a hard nut to crack.

"I gotta go pack," I replied, and tore out of the kitchen.

I fought with my emotions as I shoved clothes into my backpack. I was furious with myself for not having stuck to my original "no" to Anne. I could have stayed home.

I could have gone to prom and my recital. And yet, I knew I wouldn't have been able to think about anything else but Poppie. I would have been distracted with worry and probably about as good as useless.

"Ready?" Anne stuck her head in my room.

"Yeah, just finishing. You pack the toothbrushes?"

"Yes, and the shampoo." Anne hovered at the door. "Cassie, don't be like that."

"Like what?"

"He's different."

"They all are."

"No, I mean it. He's a good guy. I really like him. Please, Cassie, give him a chance."

"And your degree? You know the university doesn't allow profs to date students."

"They do if you sign an agreement not to sue for them for sexual harassment."

"When did you do that?" I asked, furious that she had told me nothing.

"A while back. Look, Cassie. He's a good guy. Give him a chance," she repeated.

It was the pleading in her voice that made me weaken. She gave me a crooked smile, her hands nervously twisting the edges of her jacket. I crossed the room and hugged her hard. "Just worried. About you. About Poppie."

"I know, Cassie-bug. I know," she said.

"Is there anything I can take downstairs for you?" Gunnar asked from the hallway.

Anne released me and turned to him. "Yes, I've a suitcase in the bedroom and a backpack."

"Are you taking your books?" I asked, incredulous.

"Are you taking your violin?" she retorted.

"'Nuf said." I never went anywhere without my violin. And Anne had been known to travel with a change of underwear in her purse and a suitcase full of books.

We both smiled, hearing Gunnar swear in surprise at the weight of Anne's luggage. I moved all of my plants into the bathroom, setting them in the bottom of a tub filled with about four inches of water. It wasn't much, but I figured it would keep them from drying out. The hibiscus shed her yellow pollen on the green leaves of the philodendron.

"Watch it, you two," I whispered. "No funny business in there while I'm gone."

Shouldering my backpack, I grabbed my coat and violin case. I was the last one out, so I turned the key in the lock and shoved it into my pocket. As I did, I felt the hard cube of the fiddler's rosin. I brought it out and held it up to the morning sunlight. It gleamed like amber honey and smelled tart and piney. Gold flecks and pine needles were trapped in the cube. I put it back into my pocket and hurried to catch up with Anne and Gunnar.

They were outside on the street, Gunnar stuffing the suitcases next to bags of groceries in the trunk of a shiny new black Saab. My eyebrows went up a notch and I was willing to give him a few credit points right then. Artsy, but with money. Now that was definitely new.

"Ready?" he asked me, and I couldn't tell from the cool tone in his voice whether he was asking about the trip or a fight over Anne.

"Yeah, I'm ready," I replied, and climbed into the back seat.

✦ chapter four ✦

FOR THE FIRST HOUR OF driving, I didn't say much. Gunnar and Anne talked about movies, mostly foreign ones I'd never seen. Then they had a friendly argument about a novelist whom Anne hated and Gunnar liked. I spaced and just let my mind wander as I watched the scenery roll by. There wasn't much to see at first. Just the same dreary strip malls, car dealerships, and fast-food places. Every now and then, a farmhouse appeared in an island of short grass, as if swept up and then deposited at the edge of the road. In the summer the highway's earthen shoulder would bloom with blue chicory, white stands of Queen Anne's lace, and deep patches of purple pea vetch. But now, except for the tossed litter, it was empty and muddy.

The Saab was comfortable. I sprawled in the back seat, and when their conversation trailed off, Gunnar snapped on the radio, hunting until he found a decent classical station. Nice car, and, unless it was an act to butter me up, nice taste in music. A little Bartók, some Mozart, and a few surprise pieces of Handel drowned out the steady drone of the highway. The day was really pretty, with a blue sky and a few clouds. When we got outside the city, I saw a red-tailed hawk drifting over a stand of oaks, his tail feathers splayed out in the winds. The sun streamed through Anne's window. The warmth made her drowsy and after a while she dozed off. I checked the rearview mirror and watched Gunnar, his blue-gray eyes focused on the road ahead, his hands steady on the wheel. He caught my glance and smiled back.

"Is it all right back there? The music, is it too loud? Would you like to hear something different?"

"No," I answered, "it's great. I like the music."

"Anne says you are very good on the violin. I would like to hear you play sometime."

"Sure," I said, not really believing him. Anne's boyfriends always said that at first, then complained when I practiced too much and woke them up. I smiled to myself. I'd used my violin as a weapon more than once when I was first learning. I'd known I sucked, but it didn't stop me from playing some truly annoying piece over and over until Anne's boyfriend of the month would flee the house. Anne, however, rarely complained and, even when we were really broke, always managed to find the bucks to fork over to a teacher and rent a violin.

It occurred to me then that even though our life had gone through so many changes—different cities, different schools, different part-time jobs, and different boyfriends—my violin, the farm, and Anne's writing were the constants we never abandoned.

My mother was a great storyteller. When I was really little, and the boyfriends had all been shooed home or not shown up, I snuggled in her bed at night and she spun out tales. She started out with simple stories about kittens and dogs, ponies with pink hair. But I wanted the stories that matched Poppie's drawings, full of strange creatures and the pines. It took some fussing, but when Anne finally came around I was well rewarded. She gave me rich and fanciful stories full of wonderment and botany. Girls in leafy dresses slipped into the woods at night to find healing herbs with names like coltsfoot and joe-pye. Stout-hearted heroes learned to shape-shift into animals, and ancient tamaracks lifted their roots up out of the ground, like women raising their petticoats to join in the dance at the fairy ring. And because I demanded them, there were magic rings, self-stirring spoons, and talking cows. The only thing she refused to talk about was the winter hare. "That creature belongs to your grandfather," she sniffed. When I was old enough to read, I begged for written versions that I could take to school and share on the playground. Anne started typing them out. After a while it was a habit, and she wrote a new one every month, which I read aloud bit by bit to my friends at recess. They loved them as much as I did.

"Why don't you become a writer, Anne?" I asked her one day.

"Nah," she said, and waved me away.

"Yeah, you should," I insisted.

"I don't know enough about it. And besides, it doesn't pay. You know the arts. It's feast or famine. I can't live like that."

"Why not? We've had enough practice." I laughed, then stopped as her face clouded over. "Why not go back to school?" I said, changing tactics. "You could teach and write. What other job would let you read all the time? And give you a reason to buy more books, your One True Passion?"

She had smiled at me, a light glowing in her eyes. And that was it. We moved from Sacramento, where we were living at the time, back to Rose Bay, where Anne could get in-state tuition. She took out loans, even got a couple of scholarships as a single mother, and started school. She bitched about it when papers were due, or when she was behind in her reading, or when she lost time for her own writing. But I knew how much she loved it.

And that was the real reason we hadn't been back to the farm in two years. A week after she had enrolled at the college, we went up north. Anne wanted to tell Poppie her plans, to share her good news. But his reaction was strange, even for Poppie. He cried. He had buried his face in his hands and sobbed. "Don't, Annie, don't leave me."

Anne and I had stared at each other in bewilderment. She took him in her arms, stroked his beautiful thick gray hair, and tried to soothe him.

"I won't leave you, Dad. I promise. But it's time now for me. Time to do my work."

"You said you'd come back to stay. You said you'd take care of things," he whined. "It's not safe out there."

Anne tried, but he refused to be comforted. Then he

got angry. Went into his studio and slammed the door on us. I knocked and knocked, but he wouldn't answer.

We stayed one more night at the farm. I woke early and saw him standing on the edge of Great-Grandmother Hannah's garden. The tall feathered fronds of the yarrow plants waved at him, his lips moving as he talked to someone. I went to him, hoping that he might be willing to talk now. But he kept talking to invisible people, and even when I tugged hard at his sleeve, he refused to look at me, just brushed me away as though I were a fly buzzing in his ear.

"Poppie, please," I begged. "It's me, Cassie."

He started humming a tune. He looked through me as though I wasn't even there. Then he walked past, an elbow shoving me out of the way none too gently as he made his way to the edge of the forest to stand in the shadow of the pine trees. Anne found me crouched in Hannah's garden sobbing, my hands stained green from ripping up spearmint plants. She gave me a hug, blotted my tears, put me in the car, then got our stuff together. Through the car window I could see her walk across the field to Poppie. She was talking to him, her hands gesturing angrily in the air. He never turned around. So she left him there. In Ashland she stopped at the little white church and made arrangements with Father Tom, whom she had known since grade school. He would go out there and check on Poppie and call her if there was a problem. In two years we had been back twice. And both times had been brief, painful, and no better.

"Would you like some coffee, Cassie?" Gunnar asked from the front seat. "There is a thermos in the bag back there. And some cookies if you like."

He must have thought I was like Anne, the cookie queen. Well, at least it showed he was considerate. Maybe Anne was right. Maybe this one was different. I decided to be polite. For Anne's sake.

"I'm fine, really. Can I give you some?"

"Sure, why not?"

I found the thermos and unscrewed the cap. The car filled with the aroma of coffee as I poured out a little cupful and handed it up to him.

"Thanks," he said, sipping it carefully, one hand on the wheel. "Pretty country out here. Looks almost like Sweden."

The scenery had changed a lot since we had headed into the countryside. Poppie's paintings had trained me to the habit of studying landscapes, watching carefully for the light playing across trees, the mood and tone of the land. I looked now from the windows and smiled. A faint, green mist hovered over the trees and shrubs unfolding in the distance with the warm spring sun. Blackbirds, their wings stained with crimson patches, flew to the shoulder of the highway and scratched in the gravel. Here and there were stands of willows, the long strands of yellow leaves fluttering in the wind next to poplars and aspens. The newly plowed fields were a rich brown. In the front yard of an old farmhouse, a cloud of delicate pink flowers floated around the gnarled branches of a crab apple tree. A dark rectangle of earth with tomato cages and trellises promised vegetables in the coming months. At another farm, laundry snapped on a clothesline, yellow sheets and towels at one end, a man's collection of white shirts and handkerchiefs at the other. A tire swing hanging from a spreading maple twirled in the wind.

"Is your grandfather's farm like these?" Gunnar asked as he handed me the empty cup.

"No. Ours was never really a working farm."

I don't think our farm had ever been like the ones that we were passing, domestic and tame. The few decent fields had always been rented out and most of the land had been left untouched as forest and marsh. The few cleared acres around the house were dense with long grass, and the farm's tangled heart was my great-grandmother Hannah's garden. It had no vegetables, no peas and potatoes, no lettuce. Not a single ordinary begonia or zinnia. Instead, it was overgrown with flowers that Hannah had collected from the woods and nurtured. Almost seventy years ago, she had abandoned the idea of a neat rectangle and had planted everything in a spiral maze of strange plants, some tall and heavy-headed with blossoms, others tiny, like a carpet of flowering velvet. In the fall she had harvested the seeds, storing them in carefully labeled brown envelopes all packed in old cigar boxes. As a little kid, I used to sit on the kitchen stoop, a box balanced on my knees, and rifle through the packets of seeds. I had wanted to find magic beans and plant a beanstalk that would lead me to the giant's house. But the seeds were tiny black dots, and one year I scattered a handful near the back stoop by wiping my sticky palms off on my jeans. I was rewarded the following year by a clump of blue spiderwort, its star-shaped flowers lifting over long green stalks.

"You must have enjoyed going there when you were small. My parents had a cottage in the country and every summer my mother would take us children there. My father would then come on the weekend when he was done with work. I loved it. We would swim in the ocean, explore the fields and the pines. It was great."

"I always thought being at the farm was pretty cool," I said. *Before things got too weird, anyway.* "It's beautiful, but in a messy kind of way."

I fell silent as an unexpected memory surfaced. I was a little girl, standing beside Anne, her damp hand clutching mine. She was younger, her blonde hair in loose braids. I remembered looking down and seeing the broken lace of one of her boots reknotted in two places. We were standing on the threshold of the house and the door was open wide. In the front hallway a faded rug gave up the last blooms of pale lilies along its border and the dust swirled in the slanting light of the open door. Anne was refusing to enter the house. Her fear of the place traveled like electricity through her hand into mine and I started to whimper, afraid but not knowing why.

At once, Poppie appeared from his studio down the hall and ambled toward us. He smiled at Anne and quietly touched her hair, almost as if to reassure himself that she was really there. But still she said nothing. My whimpers turned into wails. I didn't understand this strange, silent meeting. As he bent down to me, his black hair spilled across his paper-white forehead. He stroked my cheek to quiet my cries and took my other hand in his. Unlike Anne's, it was dry and warm and very inviting. He pulled me and then my mother into the house, down the hallway, past the parlor that I knew sparkled with crystal glasses in the sideboard. Lace curtains were fluttering in the breeze, casting an intricate shadow over the maroon velvet furniture.

Down the hallway we went, following my grandfather. As we passed the open door to his studio, I tugged on his hand to make him stop. I wanted to go in there. There was an easel, jars of pencils, brushes, and the strong smell of turpentine. But Poppie was pulling us, towing us eagerly to the back of the house. In the kitchen the walls were painted an ocean blue. Sunlight from the windows polished the grain of an old wooden table. Blue-and-white dishes filled the hutch, and thin slabs of orange geodes hung in the windows over the pump and the gray marble sink. Poppie pushed open the back door and we were outside again, in the brilliant green of Hannah's garden.

Poppie released my hand and, almost at once, I found the stone walk that began the garden's spiral path. I ran, following the inward curve of the path until I was lost in the very center of the garden, hidden by the tall blooming flowers. There were bees everywhere, bumbling noisily amid the blossoms, bending the flower stalks with the weight of their bodies. I looked out beyond the garden and saw Poppie, his gaze fixed on the sweeping branches of the surrounding pines. Standing in his shadow where he couldn't see her was Anne, her face downturned and full of tears.

The blast of a car horn jarred me out of my memories. The Saab swerved as a battered red sedan cut in front of us. Anne's head banged against the window and she woke, swearing.

"Idiots," Gunnar snapped. "Are you all right?" he asked Anne.

"Yeah," she answered, rubbing her temple. "What the hell was that?"

"Those jokers ahead of us."

Their rear bumper was tied on with rope and plastered with stickers that urged us to "Question Authority," "Find Your Bliss," and "Commit Random Acts of Kindness."

"How about random acts of driving?" Gunnar snorted.

I could guess where they were headed. Up to Ashland for the music festival.

"Where are we, anyway?" Anne asked me.

"About halfway," I answered.

"Let's stop soon. Maybe for some lunch. What do you think, Anne?" Gunnar asked.

"Yeah, that would be nice. There's a place up the road a bit called the Pine Knoll, where Cassie and I usually stop. It's an old-fashioned spoon. Good pies, strong coffee." She smiled, her expression still sleepy.

"Good, I'm hungry," he said as he patted her thigh.

A few minutes later, we were pulling into the parking lot of the Pine Knoll. The red sedan was there, and so were a couple of other beat-up-looking cars with bumper stickers. "U.S. Out of El Salvador," "Stop the Strip Mines," and one that didn't match at all, "I Brake for Unicorns!" I found it hard to take anyone seriously who had such a stupid bumper sticker. Anne and I had only one on our Toyota. "Girls Kick Ass." I thought that said it all.

We walked into the old diner and were greeted by the doleful gaze of the mounted deer head hung high over the counter, above the pie racks. I waved to it out of habit as the black glass eyes followed us to our booth. In one corner three tables were pushed together and a crowd of college students was talking loudly and shooting straw wrappers at one another. I had been right about their destination. Instrument cases were shoved under the table next to their feet. Liz, one of Pine Knoll's regular waitresses, was standing by the table, looking majorly pissed off as some girl with dreadlocks kept changing her mind about what she wanted while her friends shouted out suggestions.

"Look, honey, I'll just bring you something good," Liz said, and started to collect the menus.

"Um, okay. No meat though."

"Right." Liz rolled her eyes. She caught sight of us, tucked the menus under one arm, and waved.

"They know you here?" Gunnar said.

"Oh yes. Lizzie and I were in the same class at school," Anne answered.

"Really, " Gunnar remarked, a bit surprised.

Liz was as tall as Anne, but she looked a good deal older. Her hair had gone through a number of color changes over the years. It was a burnt mahogany now, cut very short around her long, slightly horsey face. Her thin eyebrows were penciled in over her blue eye shadow. Blue veins knotted up the sides of her calves, but her ankles were still slim.

"Hey, Annie Laurie, how the hell are you?" Liz called out, smiling and chewing her gum at the same time. "I haven't seen you in ages. Cassie, honey, look at you, all grown up."

"Still short," I said ruefully.

"But very, very pretty. Always loved those dark eyes of yours. You breaking hearts yet? Of course you are."

Anne introduced Gunnar, and the three of them started chatting. I stopped listening as soon as I noticed the gray-haired fiddler from the Dubliner sitting at the counter, twirling a spoon on the Formica surface. I found myself immediately hoping his wasn't the car with the damn unicorn sticker. He glanced over his shoulder and saw me. He smiled a greeting, then his gaze shifted to Anne. The spoon stopped twirling and the fiddler gave her a desperate stare. Inwardly, I sighed. It was always the same. A waitress put a cup of coffee and a piece of pie down in front of the fiddler, but he continued to stare hungrily at Anne. Then he caught himself, lowered his eyes, and set about adding sugar to the coffee.

"What'll you have, Cassie honey?" Liz asked, a hand on one hip while the other was braced on our table. Her nails were a pretty shade of coral to match her lipstick.

"A grilled cheese on whole wheat, extra pickles, and fries, please," I answered without a pause.

"As if I didn't already know that," Liz teased. "One day you'll come in and order something different and I'll just have to retire from amazement. I will have heard everything. Cassiopeia Brittman changed her order. Lord save me!"

I blushed furiously. Liz's voice was loud and the fiddler used the opportunity to look over his shoulder again.

"And you, Annie Laurie, are you going to order the usual, too?" One penciled eyebrow arched in a question.

Anne laughed. "How can I resist? Pancakes, sausage, and hash browns, and lots of syrup, please."

"Oh, Gunnar, honey, please make my day interesting," Liz said, rolling her eyes.

Gunnar had been the only one of us to read the menu.

"How about the Thursday special, pot roast?" he suggested.

Liz screwed up her face and shook her head. "Awful," she mouthed silently.

"Okay, then how about a bacon cheeseburger with everything on it, fries, and a chocolate malt."

"Fabulous." She grinned and sauntered away to the kitchen.

Gunnar slipped off his leather jacket and hung it over the back of his chair. He had on a tight black T-shirt with blue jeans and looked pretty hip.

"Cassiopeia," he repeated. "How did you get such an interesting name?"

No doubt Gunnar thought he was asking about some funny family story. Boy, what a mistake.

"Ask Anne," I said.

Anne glared at me and then smiled. "Oh, that. A friend of mine pointed out the stars one night and I just liked the sound of it. That's all, really."

A friend. That's how she identified my father. He'd been an astronomy professor, and no doubt I was conceived while he was showing off his knowledge of the night sky.

Gunnar must have sensed the awkwardness because he changed the subject. "Anne, Cassie tells me that your farm was never a working farm. How did your grandparents survive, then?"

Anne ran her hand through her hair, smoothing out a few stray tangles. "Originally it *was* intended to be a working farm. Orville Brittman, my grandfather, had purchased the land very cheaply in the early nineteen hundreds after the logging industry dried up in the north. He moved up there with Hannah and I think they must have farmed for about four or five years."

"What happened?" Gunnar asked.

"Orville left Hannah and the farm just after my father, Daniel, was born."

"Why?"

Anne shook her head, her lips pressed together. "Who knows? But after he left, Hannah survived as a country doctor. She studied traditional medicine and then planted an enormous garden of all wild medicinal plants. It was like a living pharmacy. Doctors and drugs were very scarce up north and she got a reputation for being good at sewing up gashes, setting broken bones, and curing fevers. I think that at one time, she delivered almost all of the babies that were born around there. In return for her work, people saw to it that she and Daniel had what they needed to get by. She went a little crazy living alone, but she managed pretty well."

"And your father? He didn't want to make it into a farm either?"

"God, no!" Anne exclaimed. "He tried to run as far away as he could. He moved to France, got married, tried his hand at art, but mostly failed. When he was totally broke, he came home from Europe and moved back to the farm."

"With your mother?" Gunnar asked, trying to piece it altogether.

Anne pursed her lips as if sucking on sour candy. "Yeah, with my mother, Henriette. She didn't stay, though. The farm was a little too primitive for a Parisian girl like her. Too bad, because just after she left, Daniel started doing his landscapes. They were different from the crap he had painted in France. For one thing, they were good and they made him famous. They also made him crazy."

"Crazy?" Gunnar looked surprised.

It was strange to hear Anne talk openly about our family. She usually kept our skeletons well hidden. Maybe she thought Gunnar could take it. Or maybe it was a test.

Liz came over to the table, her arms laden with plates of food.

"Here you go, darlings," she said, setting them down. From her apron pocket she pulled out extra napkins, the catsup, and a syrup bottle. "I'll get that malt and be right back. Annie, you want something to drink?"

"Coffee, please," Anne replied.

"How did your father's paintings make him crazy?" Gunnar asked again, uncovering his hamburger to squeeze a big blob of catsup on the bun.

"I don't know," Anne answered irritably. "He thought it was being at the farm that had brought him success and, therefore, he shouldn't leave the place. Ever. He wouldn't go to gallery openings, had all our groceries delivered. It was strange. I grew up alone with two stone-crazy adults, my grandmother in her garden, my father in his studio, and nothing but northern woods and swamps. As soon as I was old enough, I took off. A good thing, too, or else . . . " Her voice trailed off as she smeared butter all over her pancakes. Liz came and set down the coffee and the malt, then hurried away to the college students who were waving at her.

"Or else what?" Gunnar asked, interested.

I'd heard this complaint too often. I probably could have repeated it word for word. But it was up to Anne.

She continued spreading the butter on her pancakes.

"Or else what?" he pressed.

"Oh, I don't know." She shrugged. "It was no place to bring up a child, that's all." She picked up her fork and dug into her pancakes. Her eyes turned a dark, stormy sea green, the pale line of her eyebrows knitted together.

I knew that look. Apparently, so did Gunnar. We were both quiet, waiting for Anne to say what was on her mind.

She drew a deep breath, then exhaled, puffing out her cheeks.

"Cassie, I want to sell the farm," she said.

"What?" I asked, as shocked as if I had been slapped hard across the face.

"I think it's time to sell the farm," Anne repeated.

"You can't. You just can't." I smacked the table with my palm and the water glasses jumped.

"Calm down, Cass. Calm down. It's not an unreasonable plan. We could use the money. It would get us both through college."

"Poppie won't let you sell the farm."

Anne set her fork down and slowly wiped her lips on a napkin. "I have power of attorney to look after his affairs, Cass. I can make any decisions that I see fit. I don't need his approval."

I was so angry it was hard to swallow. "You can't sell the farm. It would kill him."

"Perhaps your grandfather is too ill to return to the farm alone. Maybe it's time to move him into the city into some kind of assisted housing for the elderly," Gunnar put in. "It's difficult, but it might be crueler to leave him where he could get seriously hurt living alone."

My temper flared. He knew. Anne had already been talking to him behind my back. About Poppie, about selling the farm. "You're just the new boyfriend. Stay out of it," I snapped. "This is between my mother and me."

Gunnar sat back, his fork and knife clanging against the rim of his plate. Irritation flashed in his eyes but he said nothing. Then he stood, the chair scraping angrily as he pushed it back. He strode off, heading in the direction of the rest rooms.

"God, you're rude," Anne said sharply. Two red spots flared on her pale cheeks. "Don't you dare screw this up for me."

"Screw things up for you! You're crazy if you think I'm going to let you sell the farm." Panic bubbled in my chest. She could do it, she could sell the farm, pack Poppie off to an old folks' home, and there was nothing I could do to stop her. Except make her life hell with arguing. "I'll get a job, I'll pay for my college myself. You don't have to sell the farm."

"Cassie, be reasonable for once. We hardly go up there anymore, and your grandfather is too old to live out there alone."

"I'll take care of him."

"No," she said sharply. "You can't. I won't let you. You have a life in front of you and it's not on the farm taking care of a mad old man."

"But the farm. Poppie. It's all we have left of our family," I insisted.

"Not much of a family," Anne said softly. Her eyes welled with tears. "A crazy man and a house full of sad memories. Loss and pain."

"Those are your memories. What about my memories? And the garden? That's *my* special place, you know that," I said desperately. "How could you sell that away from *me*?"

Anne groaned and turned her face toward the wall. "I hate it all," she whispered.

"Anne, Mom, please, can't we talk about this?" I begged.

"Say now, didn't we meet last night?" a gravelly voice interrupted.

The fiddler was standing by our table, oblivious to the fight Anne and I were having. A pleasant smile played on his lips. "You all heading up north?"

I scowled, too upset to make pleasant conversation with a stranger.

Anne turned from the wall, her face blotchy with crying. She looked at the fiddler and her eyes widened, startled.

"Thought I recognized you," the fiddler said a little smugly.

"We've never met," Anne replied, but her shoulders stiffened and her fingers curled into fists on the table.

They stared at each other silently, the fiddler rocking back on his heels. "Well, my mistake," he said, not too convincingly. He grinned at me and the white fingers raked through his gray hair. "Still got that rosin I gave you?"

"Yeah," I answered, puzzled by the whole encounter. "I still have it."

"Good, hang on to it. It's good rosin." He looked us over again, his eyes resting a moment longer on Anne. She refused to meet his glance. "So long, then," he said, and walked out of the diner slowly, moving with a strange loping gait.

"Do you know that guy?" I asked Anne.

"No," she answered curtly. "Why should I? Just because I grew up in the north woods doesn't mean I know every hayseed around. No, I have no idea who that was," she repeated.

I stared at her a moment longer, hoping for an explanation. But when Anne didn't want to talk about something, nothing could move her. She was stubborn, secretive and impossible. *Just like Poppie*, I thought.

Gunnar returned to the table, sat, and wolfed down his hamburger. We finished the meal in silence, listening only to the college students shouting and teasing one another. It was hard not to envy their happiness as I choked down my food, feeling miserable and scared. Anne couldn't sell the farm. She just couldn't. I glanced up and Gunnar had taken hold of her hand. She gave him a sad, apologetic smile. *It's not fair*, I thought. He was on her side and I had to fight alone.

When the bill came, Anne snatched it before Gunnar could. "I've got it," she said briskly, throwing down a five-dollar bill for Liz, and then heading for the cash register. Gunnar followed her, looking decidedly put out. Though we walked together, he didn't say a word to me, and I sure as hell wasn't in the mood to apologize for anything.

At the car, I climbed into the back seat again. I fumbled in my backpack for my portable CD player and pulled it out. I clamped the headphones over my ears and turned on Corelli's "La Folia." Curling into a knot, I closed my eyes and let the dark, restless violins echo my worried thoughts.

✦ chapter five ✦

I FELL ASLEEP IN THE back seat and woke later when Gunnar pulled into a gas station. Anne got out quickly and headed for the mini-mart. I went in search of the rest room.

When I came out, Anne was buying an armload of snacks and sodas. My favorites: corn chips, a can of bean dip, grape soda, and cheesy popcorn, the kind that left your fingers totally orange. It was a peace offering. She smiled wanly at me, her eyes hopeful.

"Here," she said, handing me the chips and bean dip.

"Thanks," I mumbled, and took them.

We walked out to the car as Gunnar was finishing drying off the windows.

"I just have to pay for the gas and we're off," he said, tossing the towel into the trash bin.

"I did already," Anne said, and slipped into the car.

"Anne, you don't have to," he answered, annoyed.

"Don't worry about it."

"I want to help," he said.

"Please, Gunnar, it's all right. Really. Look," she said, holding up a bag of sour-cream-and-onion chips, "your favorite. Come on, let's go."

He relented and got into the car. He glanced at me in

the rearview mirror, sitting cross-legged on the seat dipping corn chips into bean dip. Well, I might make up with Anne—after all, she was my mother and I needed to convince her she was wrong about selling the farm. But I didn't owe the Viking anything. He knew nothing about Poppie, the farm, or me. And until he did, charging in with his opinion just made him a big buttinski. So what if I'd been rude?

In the slanting afternoon light, we drove through the Eagle River Valley. I watched the landscape, tried to read it for news of Poppie. The land rolled away from the black tarred road into soft hills broken by little streams and rocky slopes. The forest sprang up around us with a varied collection of pine trees: white pines flowing like a woman's ball gown, crippled jack pines, and feathery-needled tamaracks. Beneath them were red-horned sumacs, their tall crimson spikes rising above the ferny leaves, dense blueberry bushes, and gnarled brambles. In low-lying wet patches near the road, cattails swayed and little birds perched on the stiff stalks. Occasionally, a stand of white birch trees brightened the dark wall of the forest. The sun scattered a golden light over the tops of the trees and deepened the shadows beneath the boughs.

We were close to Ashland when Anne turned to me.

"I'm sorry, Cassie. I didn't mean to upset you. Not now."

I sighed, and a knot loosened between my shoulder blades. "I'm sorry, too. I didn't mean to be difficult, but

I just freaked. Anne, please can't we talk about this? I really think selling the farm is a horrible idea."

"Why?" Anne pressed gently. "It's only a place, Cassie. We could buy a house in Rose Bay with that kind of money."

"And Poppie? You know he'll never leave."

"He may not have a choice. He's getting too old to live alone. I should have seen this coming. I should have done something sooner. I feel guilty enough about waiting this long to deal with it."

"I don't know, it still seems a bad idea to me. Look," I started to explain, "Joe's family is really straight. And there's a lot of them. Brothers, sisters, mom, dad, grandparents, and whatever. At holidays they get together and there's this big party. It's fun. They make a lot of noise, have a lot of food, and they share a lot of history together as a family. It's really cool how they all are."

Anne had been chewing her lower lip while I talked. "I've tried to make a family for you, Cassie. It's not my fault—"

"And I'm not blaming you," I said quickly. "I know you tried. But it didn't happen. Not for you, not for me, and probably not for Poppie either. But the one thing we all share is the farm. For better or worse, it's our center and the place that holds us together. When crap happened to us we always went there, didn't we? For a little while anyway. Some of my happiest memories were at the farm. I just don't want to lose it all. It means too much to me."

Anne leaned back in her seat. "I used to think like that. When I left home the first time I thought I would die, cut off from the farm. I wanted to go home but it just cost too much to stay," she said vaguely. She took a deep breath and let it out slowly. "All right, Cassie. We won't talk about selling the farm just now. Let's see how Poppie is doing. Get the old coot healthy again," she said affectionately. "If I don't have to move him I won't just yet. Though God knows I probably couldn't get anyone in there to look after him full-time. He can be such a pain in the ass. Like you," she added with a smile.

I settled back, content. I glanced at Gunnar's face in the rearview mirror and resisted the urge to look smug. I was surprised to see that he looked worried, rather than pissed off.

It was twilight when a road sign welcomed us to Ashland, and just beyond it was the sign for the hospital. When Gunnar turned the Saab down the side road, Anne retrieved a brush from her purse and began to feverishly fix her hair. I got anxious, thinking about Poppie. Anytime Anne had tried to take him somewhere off the farm, he grew very difficult. I could only imagine how they were handling him in the hospital.

"I hope I can do this," Anne blurted out.

"It'll be all right," I said, trying to convince myself, too.

Gunnar parked under the lights of the visitor's lot. I popped out of the back seat, and as soon as I straightened to standing, I heard the joints of my knees crack. Blood tingled in my cramped toes. An early mist had settled in the cool spring air and my breath hovered like a fragile cloud. I looked the hospital over, not liking the square brick box stamped with teeny windows. I could have bet it was painted lime green inside.

At the main entrance there was a little patch of grass that had not yet been mowed. Tiny purple and white violets were blooming above small, heart-shaped leaves. I bent down and quickly gathered up a small handful. Then I hurried to catch up with Gunnar and Anne.

The woman at the registration desk was too engrossed in her coffee and newspaper to notice when we came in. Her thick bifocals made her heavy green eye shadow look even worse than it was.

"May I help you?" Her eyes barely lifted from the newspaper.

"Yes," Anne said. "I'd like Daniel Brittman's room number."

"Visiting hours haven't started yet. They're between seven and eight-thirty P.M."

"We're family," Anne said.

Now the woman did look up. "Anne? Annie Brittman, is that really you? God, I haven't seen you in years."

Anne frowned, then a spark of recognition lit her face. "Nadine Franck. From high school, right?"

"It's Nadine Anderson now. I married Bill Anderson." Anne looked blank.

"You remember him, don't you? Big strong guy, blond. He did track. Took first in state. Remember?"

"I'm sorry," Anne shook her head. Nadine looked disappointed.

"Oh well. You sure look great anyway," she continued. "Haven't changed a bit," she added with a pained sigh. She turned to the computer screen at her elbow. "I expect you'll be wanting to see your father right away. Let's see." Her lower lip stuck out as she read down a list of names. "Here he is in ICU."

"Intensive care?" Anne asked sharply.

Nadine looked sympathetically over her bifocals. "'Fraid so. I don't know what the story is. They don't tell us that. But it's on the fourth floor. Just ask the charge nurse there to fill you in. You might run into Melvin up there," she added, taking off her glasses. "Melvin Steiger bought the old Pienkowski farm next to yours after George died. Melvin offered Father Tom a hand in looking after your father over the last year. Tom's mom got really ill and he had his hands full taking care of her." Nadine's voice sharpened slightly. "'Course now that you're here, maybe you'll stay awhile and look after your father yourself."

It was an accusation, not a suggestion. *You don't care about your father*, it said. *You're irresponsible.* But it really wasn't about that at all. It wasn't fair that Anne could leave the farm, leave the north, then return looking nearly as good as the day she left. Nadine's envy was as green as her eye shadow.

"Good to see you, too," Anne said curtly.

She strode quickly for the elevators, Gunnar and I

hurrying to catch up. Anne stabbed at the call button.

"Forget it," Gunnar soothed, taking her hand.

"That woman has no idea who I am. Or what I have done to keep body and soul together," Anne said bitterly.

The doors to the elevator hissed open. I hit the '4' button and felt my stomach lurch with the bumpy upward ride. And as the doors slid open at the fourth floor with a ping, I saw the walls were indeed lime green.

My heart rapped nervously as we followed the signs to the ICU. I had to remind myself to breathe, even though I felt like gagging on the antiseptic hospital smell. Anne stepped up to a long desk lined with TV monitors and beeping machinery. A young nurse in scrubs looked up from her paperwork.

"I'm Anne Brittman. I've come to see my father."

"Oh yes." The young woman smiled. "There's a note in his chart that you might be in town today. I'm Mr. Brittman's night nurse. He's in room 428. I think he's resting pretty comfortably now. They did give him a sedative earlier because he was very agitated and fighting the respirator—"

"Respirator?" Anne broke in anxiously.

"Yes. He came in with pneumonia and was having difficulty breathing due to the fluids in his lungs. But he seems to be responding to the medication and his lungs are finally draining. We have him up here in ICU because he is an older gentleman and his system in general is weaker. His heart and kidneys may have been compromised by his illness."

Anne paled. "Will he be all right?"

"It'll take a few days to be certain. But I've seen some come in here looking far worse than your father and then walk out a month later. He's definitely fighting it," she said encouragingly. "You can go in and see him if you want. But just for a few minutes."

Nervously, we entered Poppie's hospital room. It was dim, barely lit through the curtained window that looked into the corridor of the ICU. I was dazed at first by the sight of so many machines humming and clicking, blinking with red digital numbers to the rhythm of his breathing. A web of plastic tubing from different IVs drained through needles that were buried in the backs of Poppie's hands and the soft inner skin of his elbow.

Anne stifled a moan, a hand over her mouth. Poppie was tall and thin, his shoulder blades jutting from his back like the wings of a hawk. He had walked with a powerful, long-legged stride, his arms swinging loosely at his sides. He had been handsome, with his fierce green eyes, a sharp nose, and a clean jaw.

Now he lay like a spindled ghost, as fragile as dust. He was so pale he was almost transparent. I could almost see where the medicine entered his blue veins and traveled up his arm. His eyes were half closed, exposing only a thin rim of green around huge black pupils dilated from the sedatives. The respirator tube was taped to his opened mouth, his dry lips chapped. I touched his shoulder fearfully and felt the vibrations of the machine that forced air into his lungs. Pushing aside the tubes, I took his hand. Tears were brimming in my eyes as I saw that the nurses had not been able to scrub away the ink stains.

Anne was crying quietly, one hand holding tightly on to Gunnar, the other gently stroking Poppie's chest.

The machines clicked and whirred, and the noise from the corridor seemed too loud. I bent over the railing of the bed and leaned down close to Poppie's ear.

"Poppie, it's me, Cassie, and Anne."

The eyes flickered, moved back and forth beneath the wrinkled lids. A machine responded with a beep and new numbers flashed across its digital face. I felt the sticklike fingers of his hand move very weakly in mine.

"I brought you flowers, Poppie. Violets." The hand squeezed mine again. His eyes stopped moving and looked at my face. I tried to smile.

"I'll get some water for them. So you can have them in here," I offered.

I let go of his hand and found a paper cup over the sink. I filled it with water and let my tiny bouquet of violets rest inside. They drooped over the sides, but in that alien hospital room, I knew they possessed a power to inspire my grandfather that was lost in those machines designed to keep him alive. I placed them on the table beside his bed, where he would see them when the sedative had worn off.

Anne was huddled into Gunnar's shoulder, weeping silently. Gunnar and I exchanged glances, a shared moment of agreement. He steered her toward the door.

"Come on, Anne, it's time to go now. We'll come back later."

"Wait," she said. She bent over the bed's railing and kissed Poppie softly on the forehead. After a moment, she allowed Gunnar to lead her out of the room. I waited at the end of Poppie's bed, still trying to accept the strange sight of him adrift in the cold sea of white sheets. My chest hurt as if the pneumonia were clogging up my own lungs.

I felt light-headed and closed my eyes to keep my balance. As I did I thought I saw a small pointed face in the corner of the room, with huge dark eyes and a nose of twisted wood, like one of the creatures in Poppie's drawings. When I opened my eyes, the face disappeared. The IV tubes trembled. I stepped away from the bed, a little freaked by my overactive imagination, but also comforted by the idea that maybe he wasn't alone. He had brought someone from the farm to be with him.

The nurse appeared at the door. "I have to ask you to leave now. There are some things I need to do for Mr. Brittman."

"Can we call you later?" I asked. "Just to find out how he's doing?"

"Sure," she said, moving over to the IV stand and replacing the nearly empty bag with a fresh one. She caught sight of the violets and reached to remove them.

"Please," I said, stopping her. "They're small, but it would mean a lot to my grandfather to see them when he wakes up."

"Well . . ." She hesitated. "I really shouldn't. We don't allow flowers in ICU. But I guess they can't hurt tonight." She looked up at the numbers on Poppie's machines and gave a smile. "His oxygen flow is improving."

"Great," I said, relieved. "And thanks."

I turned to leave and collided with someone coming in the doorway. A man in a dark brown jacket backed up in alarm. My nose wrinkled at the sharp odor of wood smoke and wet earth.

"Who are you?" he demanded.

"Who are you?" I demanded back.

"This is Melvin Steiger, your grandfather's neighbor," the nurse said. "He's been looking after things while your grandfather's in the hospital."

"I'm Cassie Brittman, Daniel's granddaughter," I said politely. "My mother and I just got here."

"Little late, ain't you?" he growled. "I've been here all night already."

Just thinking of him near Poppie made me queasy. He had a wide, sloping forehead and a chin covered with sandpapery black stubble. Beneath the jacket he was wearing a faded plaid shirt. His pant legs had oil stains and his boots were streaked with dried mud. How could the hospital have let such a scrub in here? I wondered. The hair on my arms prickled.

But the nurse was just smiling at him, as if he were the most pleasant creature on earth. What had Father Tom seen in this guy?

"The nurse says he's doing better," I said flatly. "But he needs to rest, so we all gotta get out of here."

"Now wait a minute," he protested. "You can't just waltz in here and tell me what to do. I don't take orders from a sassy girl. He's been in my charge up to now, you know."

"She's right, though," the nurse spoke up. "Mr. Brittman has had a rough day and is finally resting. You need to all leave, even you, Melvin."

"I'll leave the number of the farm at the desk," I said to the nurse, trying to ignore the creep steaming next to me. "Call us if . . . " I paused awkwardly.

"Just leave the number," the nurse said reassuringly. "We always call if things get bad."

"You staying out at the farm?" Melvin demanded. His eyes narrowed.

"Yeah. It's *my* home," I answered.

I waited until he had backed out of the room, then followed, heading for the elevator where Anne and Gunnar waited for me. Anne's face was buried in her hands. Gunnar had his arm around her shoulder.

"Anne," I called. "This is Melvin Steiger, the guy Father Tom let look after Poppie." It was hard not to keep the disgust out of my voice.

And Anne couldn't hide the look of dismay when she saw Melvin. Gunnar gave the guy a smile. Was he blind? Couldn't he see the guy was a creep? Anne put her hand on Gunnar's arm and stopped him from extending his hand.

"Thank you for your help," she said stiffly. "It was good of you to keep an eye on my father."

Melvin said nothing, but his eyes shifted uneasily back and forth between the three of us. Gunnar was still smiling like an idiot.

We were silent as we stepped into the elevator, the smoke-and-earth smell of Melvin's clothes suffocating in the enclosed space. I saw Anne turn away and surreptitiously cover her nose with her hand.

Once outside the hospital in the cold, damp air, Melvin turned to us.

"It's rough out at that farm. I don't reckon you should stay there."

"What do you mean by rough?" Anne asked coldly.

"Things is changed. Don't say I didn't warn you," he grumbled as he shambled away across the parking lot. He got into an old black pickup truck, started the engine with a loud roar, and squealed out the exit.

Anne exhaled hard as though she'd been holding her breath.

"Can I take the back seat, Cassie?" she asked in a tired voice. "I'm exhausted. You know the way to the farm as well as I do."

"Yeah, go ahead, lie down. I'll wake you when we get there."

As I got into the front passenger seat of the Saab, I saw that the mist had condensed on the windshield into a beautiful pattern of ferns and spirals. Under the streetlights the pattern glistened and changed even as I watched it, like a slowly turning kaleidoscope.

"What is it?" Gunnar asked.

"Nothing," I said as he turned over the motor. If he couldn't see something as ugly as Melvin Steiger standing in front of him, he sure wasn't going to recognize anything this beautiful, either. He flicked a lever and the windshield wipers pushed away the silvery pattern.

We had to go through Ashland to get to the farm. Usually a sleepy, one-street town, the place was jumping with traffic and people coming to attend the folk festival. We passed the big park in the center of town and saw tents everywhere. Banners were strung up announcing everything from "Save the Whales" to "Eat More Fruit." It had a carnival atmosphere, only without the midway and the rides. But there were dogs with red bandannas around their necks running in friendly packs, guys juggling on street corners, and little knots of musicians already sitting down to play beneath the streetlamps. On one whole side of the park people were setting up stalls for vegetables, bottled water, hemp clothing, beaded jewelry, and wind chimes. It looked fun. And I hoped that Genie had made it up here after all. Looking at the loose crowds of boys and girls strolling along, I knew this was definitely her scene. I rolled down the window a little just to catch the sound of runaway tunes, sorely needing their cheerful abandon.

We stopped at a little grocery store Anne and I always used, and loaded up on what we each considered essentials. Gunnar bought cigarettes, tea, bread, butter, cheese, some fresh vegetables, and all sorts of baking stuff like flour, sugar, and lard. That surprised me. A guy like that, I figured him for cocktail onions, steaks, and bottled salad dressing. Anne woke up long enough to get two bags of cookies, some candy bars, and milk. I got cans of soup, apples, and a box of crackers. Anne and Gunnar fought quietly at the counter as to who was going to pay for it. I decided not to stick around for that one and went to wait for them on the street with an apple.

It was strange to be standing there, so miserable and worried, while the world around me was preparing for a good time. Someone tossed a string of firecrackers into the air and little stars exploded. A flute was playing a shrill tune that almost made me shiver. I heard the roar of a motorcycle, and turned to see three riders stopped down the street at a light, shouting at one another over the idling engines. I was just able to make out the white letters on the back of one of the riders—BOG. He was here, too. How weird was that? The light changed and he roared away, taking the sound of the maddening flute with him.

"Come on, Cassie. Let's get out of here before this town gets any crazier," Anne said, a small plastic bag of groceries hanging from her arm.

We drove slowly through the traffic jams around the city square and finally turned off onto the country road leading to the farm. The city lights vanished and the night was dark again outside the car windows. Low stars twinkled between the branches of the tamaracks. A full white moon lifted over the few fields. By the time I had steered Gunnar down the dirt road to the farm, the moon had cracked like an eggshell into white shards scattered over the tall treetops.

The farm road was dark and very rough, twisting around the old trees. The Saab bounced as Gunnar drove it over deep, muddy ruts, swerving to avoid the tree trunks that seemed to put themselves suddenly in our way. Only by the pale moonlight washing over the slanting roof of the farmhouse was I able to get my bearings. The dirt road gave way to a gravel patch not far from the house. With a grateful sigh, Gunnar parked the car where I pointed, near a stand of bristling jack pines. As the motor turned off, I smiled, rolling down the window and catching the scent. In the quiet, I listened for my favorite sound, the soft brushing of the pines in the evening breeze. It meant that I was home again.

✦ chapter six ✦

THE FARMHOUSE WAS SET BACK in the shelter of the woods, only the shingled roof reflecting the moonlight. As I looked out the window of the Saab, I could tell that Melvin was right. The farm had changed. The front door was hard to see beneath the shadow of the old porch. The porch itself had broken railings and the wooden stairs were warped. The clapboard sides had been pulled off in places, revealing the wooden ribs of the house. I looked past the house at what remained of the original farm buildings. A fire, years ago, had all but destroyed the barn. The silo was a crumbling tower covered with fox grapevines. The henhouse roof had collapsed, and the structure leaned dangerously to one side. Without my grandfather there, the whole place seemed abandoned.

As I got out of the car, I was struck by the surprising quiet. There were no night sounds of animals rustling in the underbrush, no owls or wood doves calling, no chirping of crickets. Even the whooshing of the wind through the pines was stilled.

Anne stood, hands on her hips. She felt it, too. Something was wrong. The moonlight bleached her skin, and her profile was a sharp line against the shadowed forest. She started walking toward the house.

Gunnar and I took the bags of groceries from the trunk. I slipped my violin case over my shoulder and followed more cautiously.

Anne's footsteps were hollow thuds on the warped stairs. She pushed open the front door and hesitated, listening, one foot on the threshold. Then she screamed and ducked, her arms clasped protectively over her head.

A swarm of bats poured from the doorway, their leathery wings beating furiously as they squeaked in alarm.

"Get down!" I shouted to Gunnar, who lost no time in crouching by the stump of an old box elder.

I squatted by the side of the car, the groceries crushed against my chest. The air above me was thick with a muddy stream of black wings. I yelled as a bat plucked wildly at my hair, blindly waved my arm above me to fend it off.

Then, at once, they were all gone, swallowed up by the trees. The forest was quiet and the moon shone down again out of a clear night sky.

I stood slowly, wondering what else was going to come at me out of the dark house. Anne was inside, swearing loudly, and though I was scared, I ran to the steps.

"Damn it, damn it all," she yelled. There followed a wood-splitting crash and the shimmering tinkle of broken glass. Anne reappeared at the door, rigid with rage. "There's junk everywhere and the lights are out. Someone must have blown the fuses. Wait here for me," she commanded. "I'll bring out some candles. If there are any left." Then she disappeared again and I heard her cursing and shoving things in the hallway.

Then it was quiet. Very quiet. Gunnar and I looked at each other worriedly.

"I think we should go in," Gunnar said, shifting the bag of groceries to his other arm.

I followed him up the stairs, and stopped at the threshold. The air that drifted out was moist and reeked of rotting garbage and animal musk. The porch was littered with droppings, rabbit pellets, bat guano, and the skeletons of little animals. Moss covered the spindles of the porch railing, barely concealing gouges in the rotting wood. Muddy bird nests were clumped along the eaves. I saw two bats hanging upside down, their wings folded tightly over their furred bodies. They were staring back at me with glittering black eyes and squeaking with irritation.

"Anne?" I called out.

"Anne, are you all right?" Gunnar shouted.

A soft yellow light filled the hallway. I could understand now why Anne had warned us outside. There were large black forms that I realized were stacks of boxes and broken pieces of furniture. I could just make out a chair without its seat, the drawers to a chest filled with papers and bottles, and yellowed newspapers bundled with twine. A mason jar had shattered, leaving a path of broken glass. I looked down and discovered, to my alarm, that small oak saplings had split the wooden floorboards and were growing in the hallway. The old rug with its faded flowers had disintegrated into threads. I heard Anne sobbing inside the parlor.

Gunnar and I pressed into the house, pushing piles of wreckage out of our way. A flutter of wings told me that still more bats were fleeing the upper floors. Anne's cries grew louder.

"Anne? Anne! What is it? Are you all right?" Gunnar and I called. I stumbled over a pile of books and he caught me before I could fall. Together, we entered the candlelit parlor.

Then we stopped as Anne's candle cast a weak, flickering light over the walls.

"Oh, my God," I whispered, slowly taking in the terrible vision. "Oh, my God," I said again.

The room had been completely destroyed. The Persian carpets were covered with red mud and black sludge. The maroon velvet furniture had been slashed and the stuffing turned inside out. Mice and other small animals were nesting in the gutted furniture, and I could see the last inches of a long, hairless tail disappear as the candlelight passed over its hiding place. The crystal glasses were smashed on the floor, along with the old china dishes from the sideboard, whose doors had been torn off.

The lace curtains were dirty cobwebs plastered against the cracked windows. Something black shadowed the walls along the window sashes. I went closer and discovered thick, pillowy shelves of black mushrooms. Speechless, I put my arm around Anne and we stood trembling in the ruins.

"Oh, Cassie," she sobbed, "how could he live here? When did it get so bad? How could I have let this happen to him?"

As Anne and I held on to each other, Gunnar took another candle and set about inspecting the rest of the house.

"It's all my fault," Anne muttered. "But last time I was here it wasn't like this. I just don't understand. How could it all have fallen apart so quickly?"

"Anne, Cassie, come into the studio," Gunnar called.

We picked our way carefully out of the parlor, not daring to touch anything. A black pine snake slithered out from beneath the broken furniture and quickly rehid itself under a pile of split cushions. Anne shuddered and I pushed her toward the hallway.

Gunnar leaned out of the door to the studio and urged us along. "Come look," he said, and he was smiling as he took Anne's hand.

"Oh, thank God," I heard her say.

As I stepped into the room my shoulders relaxed for the first time since we had arrived. I settled the violin case alongside a neat stack of canvases all wrapped in brown butcher's paper and tied with string. I looked around the room. It was the studio I remembered. The wallpaper was dry, the pattern of white flowers on a gray background faded but clean. Some of Poppie's paintings hung on the walls. On a dresser sat jars of pencils and brushes beside a stack of black bound sketchbooks tied together with a red ribbon. A collection of acorns filled a cut-glass dish. Bouquets of dried lavender and yarrow hung around the window. A couch bed had been made up with sheets and wool blankets. A pieced quilt lay folded at one end. The room was chilly, but at least it felt alive.

"Cassie, look," Anne said, standing beside Poppie's easel.

It held a nearly finished pencil drawing of Anne and me. Anne was standing in Hannah's garden, the light dappling the fabric of her long skirt and loose blouse. Her hair flowed to her waist as it had ten years ago. Poppie had caught her sad, shy smile, the one I recognized as my mother's true smile. In one hand she held a sheaf of heartsease, a flowering grass that grew in a nearby meadow. I held her other hand, and in the drawing he had crowned me with a wreath of summer flowers, harebells and tiger lilies. I was seven, small and slim as a new cattail. I wasn't smiling but looked out at the viewer with dark, serious eyes. The breath caught in my throat. That was the year I learned for certain that Anne needed me far more than her on-again, off-again boyfriends, the waitress jobs, and the ugly cities we had run away to. I took the job seriously. How could Poppie have seen it so clearly? How could my grandfather, distracted by voices in the pines, have known what was in me?

I stepped closer to this portrait of our hidden selves. Poppie had framed us beneath the arch of a pair of queenly white pine trees. Smaller jack pines and tamaracks filled out the rest of the forest. My eye caught the faint image of a man penciled lightly in gray between the jack pines. I peered closer, only to see that it wasn't Poppie; the man leaning against the tree was playing a fiddle. He looked oddly like the fiddler from the Dubliner, gray hair sweeping over his collar, his long fingers on the neck of the violin. As I peered closer I could just make out the carved scroll with its female face. Had the fiddler known Poppie after all? Well enough that Poppie would have included him in this drawing?

"What does it mean?" I asked Anne.

"That whatever else failed him, he managed in this room at least," Anne said. "Look." She pointed to a small flat disk hung over the lintel, etched with tumbling hares. "He kept this for good luck. Protection, perhaps. He must have felt safe in here."

Gunnar was filling the black potbellied stove with loose twigs and kindling from the wood box. On top of this he carefully stacked knotted logs of oak. "We can warm up this room and stay in here tonight." He took out a box of matches from his coat pocket and lit the delicate twigs first. They sparked and a small fire bloomed.

"Are you sure you want to?" Anne asked.

"Sure, why not?"

"Well, it's a disaster here." She gestured weakly to the dark hallway. "There's so much junk in the way."

"We'll deal with that in the morning," Gunnar said with a smile.

Anne nodded, but I knew she was worried. She liked

Gunnar, and he was being pretty cool about everything so far. She had taken a chance bringing him up north. But even she had not been prepared for this. Would it be too much for him?

"Look, Gunnar, I'm really sorry," Anne said weakly. "Had I known what it was going to be like, I would never have—"

"Anne, don't worry." He stopped her. "Really, I don't scare off that easily. And remember, you don't know my family. Yet," he added with a grin.

Anne sat down on the bed, her face haggard. "God, I'm so tired." She leaned back into the pillows.

My stomach grumbled loudly and I realized I was hungry. Gunnar heard it, too, and gave me a quick nod.

"I'll try the kitchen," he said. "Maybe I can find a decent spot to cook up some soup and make sandwiches. I could use a smoke, too, to kill the smell of this old house."

"And tea," Anne muttered into a pillow, her eyes closing. "I need tea," she said to him as he headed out to the car.

Anne pulled her legs up on the bed and folded her arms across her chest. I knew that when the going got tough, she shut down and went to sleep for a little while. I paced around the room, picking things up and putting them down without really seeing them while Anne drifted into slumber. I heard Gunnar coming back in and felt a pang of guilt. Maybe he was a decent guy. Maybe I'd really been rude to him at the restaurant. Maybe I did owe him an apology. He certainly wasn't crashing and burning on us.

The fire had caught in the old stove, and already the room was warming up nicely. I grabbed the pair of candlesticks by the bed and went into the hall.

"Let me help you," I offered as Gunnar, arms full of groceries and a backpack, was shouldering his way through the cluttered hallway.

"Great," Gunnar huffed under his burden, and handed me a bag.

The kitchen was almost as bad as the parlor and hallway. We managed to clear off piles of shredded newsprint, bags crammed with other bags, and assorted junk from the countertops in order to make a place for the groceries. The woodstove was covered with a thick film of grease and soot, and the marble sink was cluttered with rusting cast-iron pots. The pump handle creaked and gasped dryly as I tried it. We cleared the kitchen table, and I found two chairs with all four legs still intact. I was relieved to see a few bowls and plates on the top shelf of the hutch. In a cupboard I found three unmatching dirty cups. There were also crackers that mice had been eating, and a jam jar with green and orange mold. There was a fridge in the corner, but Gunnar and I mutually decided to avoid it. For tonight, anyway, we were better off not knowing what was in there.

I opened a drawer and found some of the old farm utensils, long-tined forks with bone handles, soup spoons, and three knives, one badly nicked along the blade. In the next drawer down I was thrilled to see the necessary can opener, a plastic soup ladle, and a church key. Finally, I pulled out a dusty set of linen napkins with Hannah's monogram embroidered in the corners.

"I'll go out to the well and see if I can pull up some water to prime the pump," I told Gunnar. "Once the seals are dampened again, it should work."

"Is there a john in the house, or do we use an outhouse?" he asked.

"The outhouse is over there by those ash trees, but I'm not sure how safe the building is anymore. There is a john behind the closed door opposite the studio. Poppie had it put in during the fifties. Hannah didn't like it, so I'm told."

"Well, maybe I'll take a peek later," Gunnar said, lighting up a cigarette. "But now let me get this fire going in the stove," he said, opening the grate.

"Gunnar," I said, and he turned and looked at me, his expression neutral. "Look, about what I said at the restaurant. I'm sorry. I didn't mean to be rude, but nothing is that simple for us."

His eyes softened. "That's all right. I shouldn't have said anything. You're right, it really isn't my place. I thought I was helping, but I can see there is much about your lives that I don't really know."

I gave a dry laugh and looked around the battered kitchen. "Well, don't go by this. This is weird, even for us."

Gunnar smiled around the cigarette, squinting from the smoke. "Yeah. Let's just see what happens here. But for now, truce?"

"Yeah, truce," I answered, and turned to leave for water.

But before I could leave the kitchen, I had to fight to get the back door open. It was stuck, the wood swollen with dampness. It shivered opened at last, groaning, and I found myself on the back stoop once more. The bucket for the well was sitting on the bottom step next to a pot of withered johnny-jump-up pansies. I stood on the stoop and breathed in the pine-scented night air. The moonlight fell over Hannah's garden and I gazed at it, remembering running the curved path into its tangled center.

Even by moonlight, I could tell that her garden, too, had been ravaged. It looked like someone had driven through it, tearing deep ruts across the spiral pattern. My fists clenched as Melvin Steiger and his pickup truck rose in my mind. "Creep. Big creep," I said hotly as I came down the steps and threaded through the long field grass. I reached the edge of the garden and felt the anger swell, staring at its wounds. "Is this how you look after Poppie, Melvin?" I asked aloud. "Destroy his house and his garden?" Why would he do that?

But it was impossible not to feel guilty as well as angry. Anne and I hadn't called or been to see him in so long. I grew cold. All this damage had occurred to the farm within two years. The strange saplings growing in the hallway, the mushrooms against the wall, the furniture ripped apart, and our things smashed everywhere. Melvin Steiger wasn't just neglectful and sloppy. He was destructive on purpose, and it scared me that I had no idea why.

A branch cracked in the woods and my head snapped up at the sound. "Deer," I whispered, but tightened my grip on the handle of the bucket. My eyes strained to see into the dark forest, and I thought I glimpsed something white flitting through the bushes. I continued walking, and by the time I reached the well I was trembling. I hauled on the ropes, the pulleys groaning as they hoisted a second bucket from down below filled with cold water. The wind fluttered the leaves of the shrubs and I could almost imagine the little faces of Poppie's sketches appearing in the cross-hatching of twigs and moonlight.

I poured the well water into my bucket. Then I turned and saw the bright glow of eyes near my ankle.

I yelled, startled, and the green eyes blinked and jumped back. A badger crouched low to the earth hissed angrily at me. I stood completely still, the bucket handle digging a line across my palm. The badger hesitated, sniffing the air, his eyes watching me keenly. He dug a furrow in the damp soil with long silvery claws and released the scent of mushrooms and decaying leaves.

"Sorry," I mumbled to the fierce face. He growled a warning that faded into a soft chucking noise of annoyance.

I remained motionless until he shambled away, the arrow of white fur on his forehead and his snowy collar bristling in the moonlight.

"Are you all right?" Gunnar called from the back door.

My hand on my chest to steady my racing heart, I started laughing.

"Yeah, I just got spooked by a badger," I replied. First a hare, and now a badger. I had been away from the farm too long. I was starting at animals just like any city girl.

But as I returned to the house, choosing my steps carefully, it occurred to me that it was the first time I had ever been afraid on the farm. It wasn't the badger, maybe not even the unexpected swarm of bats, I decided. Melvin Steiger's beastly-looking face, his growl, and his hostility came back to me. It was him I needed to worry about. He wanted something from our land. He wanted to hurt Poppie, not care for him. I needed to talk to Anne about him. Something had to be done to keep him away.

At the back door I took one more glance at the garden and decided to tackle it in the morning. Wildflowers were hardy, and with a bit of work, I might be able to clean up and restore part of the garden. That would please Poppie when he came home from the hospital, I thought. And it might send a message to that creep Melvin to stay away.

✦ chapter seven ✦

IN THE KITCHEN, I WAS happy to discover that
Gunnar had a decent fire going and had cleared away the
pots in the sink. He had buttered pieces of bread and
they were waiting on a paper towel next to slices of
Havarti cheese. Tomato slices were frying in a little olive
oil with garlic and parsley. The smell of wood smoke and
cooking garlic took the edge off the rancid odor of the
kitchen and reminded me how hungry I was. I smiled,
surprised that he had managed to find garlic and olive oil
in Ashland's tiny grocery store. On the sink was a garlic
press, and I stared at it, my grin growing wider.

"Where did this come from?" I asked, picking it up.

"I brought it," he said, turning the frying tomatoes
gently in the pan with an old knife.

"Do you always travel with a garlic press?"

"Yeah, and some coffee filters, olive oil, and Tabasco
sauce. I've traveled to many places where these things
made the difference between a decent meal and one that
tasted like cardboard."

"You're one of those professor types, right? So how
did you get so handy?"

He laughed. "I had an aunt in Sweden with traveling
feet. She could never stay in one place for long. She wan-

dered all over the world and made her living writing travelogues. I think I became a filmmaker at the university because it was the only way to keep alive all those vivid images she filled me with as a boy. She had been in many tight spots and succeeded by being handy, as you say, intelligent, and completely at home in chaos. I guess I wanted to be like her. Of course, some Swedes are very proper and she could be like that, too, shaking out the sheets every morning, polite when looking at plates of unrecognizable food. But she had a quirky sense of humor and fun that I loved as a boy. And she had the most intimidating blue eyes I have ever seen."

"What happened to her?" I asked.

"Mostly she came and went, like a season," he said. "And then I grew up, traveled, went to college and then graduate school in America. I didn't see her for a long time. When I returned to Sweden it seemed to me that overnight, she had turned into a frail, old woman." He picked up his cigarette from the edge of the counter and took a quick puff. "It shocked me," he said softly. "I went away thinking she would never change, and returned to find her ancient. She was tiny, her hair fine, white silk. But those eyes," he said with a laugh. "They were still so blue."

"Is that why you came with Anne?"

He nodded. "Yes. Seeing people you love in the hospital is always hard."

"Is your aunt still alive?"

He shook his head and set his cigarette back down on

the counter. "No. And I miss her very much." He gave me a thoughtful look and smiled, then turned back to his tomatoes. "So, these are almost done, do we have water for the soup?"

I poured my bucket of water down the sink and listened to it gurgle deep under the counter. I worked the handle on the pump, wincing at the noise. A cough of rusted water poured out of the spout. I kept pumping until the groans had subsided into squeaks and the water flowed clean and cold into the sink. Gunnar mixed up a pan of chicken noodle soup, and I put water on the stove for tea and washing up. When it boiled, I cleaned the dishes we needed.

Gunnar set the cheese on the slices of bread and then topped them with cooked tomato slices that were soft and glistening with oil. We carried our meal into the studio and set it down on the small bedside table. Anne woke, uncurling herself like a cat, and smiling gratefully.

"Is there milk?" she asked, dipping her tea bag into the hot water.

"I'll get it," I offered. I stopped in the kitchen doorway, for by the light of Hannah's candlesticks I distinctly saw a face outside peeking through the window over the sink. This time I couldn't put it down to my tired imagination. The candle flames spluttered from a draft and shadows chased around the kitchen walls. Steam from the boiling water had condensed on the glass, making it hard to get a clear view of the face. But I saw it. It was small, like one of Poppie's comic faces, bug-eyed with curiosity, an acorn cap slid to one side. Two dark eyes flickered over everything in the room with interest. Then the eyes caught mine and they widened with alarm. The face disappeared, leaving a dark, empty oval in the wreath of steam. I ran to the window to peer out. There was no one, just the trees brushing their shadows over Hannah's garden.

Yet I could hear the frantic scrabbling of claws. Was it outside or inside, between the walls? I wondered, following the scratching sounds as they climbed up the side of the kitchen wall. As the noise moved across the ceiling I relaxed, realizing it was probably no more than a raccoon that had been attracted by the smell of Gunnar's cooking. And like everything else wild in this house, it probably had a nest between the floors. I chose to ignore the memory of the face that had seemed moments ago very familiar.

In the studio, Gunnar was stroking Anne's cheek and murmuring softly to her. I felt a bit awkward, to say the least. I was beginning to like him, but then, I had actually liked some of Anne's earlier boyfriends. But even if Anne allowed herself from time to time to rely on them, I never did. Seeing Gunnar with her now, I wanted to believe that he might be as cool as he seemed, might be unique enough to want to stay. And seeing them cuddle made me really miss Joe. I could have used a hug from my own sweetie right then.

I handed Anne the milk and then took my plate, my mouth watering at the pungent smell of garlic. I quickly took a bite of my sandwich. I closed my eyes as the tastes of cheese and warmed tomato seemed to melt together.

"Good. Really good," I mumbled with my mouth full.

"Thanks," Gunnar answered, and tore into his own sandwich.

For a while no one spoke, just ate sandwiches and slurped noodles out of the soup. It was hard not to think about what was happening. I searched the studio for signs, clues that might help me understand what had gone wrong. But there was nothing, just my grandfather's usual things, bits and pieces of the woods laid out like a still life on the windowsills and tables, a pinecone, a piece of gnarled wood in the shape of a dove, seed pods. These were mingled with Hannah's stuff: odd bits of crocheted lace, crystal dishes, a calling card with a velvet border and a picture of two hands clasped in friendship. There was a messy stack of unopened mail, some of it from Poppie's agent, no doubt, the rest from admirers hoping to get a reply from the master. A purple envelope caught my eye, and I pulled it from the bottom of the stack.

It was the letter I'd written almost six months earlier, still unopened. I felt heavy and sad. There was a time when he wrote to me. Little things, like what had bloomed that day, long Latin words I learned to memorize, or what animal he saw in the woods. Sometimes it was no more than three lines. But there were always drawings around the edges; woodland flowers and the quirky wood creatures that, even as I got older, I still loved. I knew that he had really forgotten me when even the letters had stopped coming. I held up the purple envelope for Anne to see. She grimaced, understanding. Then she flushed pink with anger.

"What the hell happened?" Anne demanded.

"You know how he is," I answered. I felt guilty, too, but also angry. There was my unopened letter in my hand, proof that I had tried, proof that he had rejected me again. "He stopped talking to us."

Anne shook her head. "He called me."

"He called you?" I repeated, astonished. "When?"

"About four months ago."

"What did he say?"

Anne shrugged. "Nothing, really. He had seen a fox crossing the snow. He had dreamed of Hannah. He wondered if the spring would come again." Anne's voice choked. "I should have known. This time was coming, but I didn't want to face it." She gazed around the room, clearly struggling with herself. "I want to sell it. Sell the damn place and never come here again."

"No!" I shouted, furious.

"You don't understand," she said in frustration. "This isn't going to get better. There's too much other stuff going on here. I should have known."

"What other stuff? Tell me!" She was holding something back, I could see it in her face, in the way her eyes refused to meet mine.

I sat there mindlessly stirring my tea. Poppie had called her, but he hadn't answered my letter. He had called her but she had never told me. Jealousy and anger warred with sadness. He wrote *me* letters, not those important people; he talked to *me*, not the agents and art critics, sometimes not even Anne. He remembered me when he forgot all the others. Or so I had thought.

I made a bed out of some spare blankets from the studio closet. They smelled cleanly of cedar and I huddled deeply in their folds. Gunnar blew out the candles and I gazed at the ceiling, watching the orange glow from the woodstove transform the white wallpaper flowers into flaming poppies. I'd talk to Anne tomorrow. Alone, without Gunnar. Maybe that way she'd open up to me. I fell asleep watching as the flowers waved their heavy heads in the shifting firelight.

✦ ✦ ✦

I couldn't say what woke me later, whether it was the grinding rattle of the motor, or the ribbon of white light from the window. But the two joined together and I recognized the growl of a motorcycle engine and the beam of its headlamp casting light into the room. I sat up, dazed by sleep, but somehow afraid. Anne was sleeping on the couch and Gunnar was snoring from a makeshift bed of two pushed-together chairs. I was about to wake them when the headlamp was abruptly shut off and the room returned to darkness. The motor died and there was quiet once more.

I heard the scrunch of footsteps as someone crossed the gravel driveway and walked toward the house. My heart was hammering, and I pressed myself against the wall. Gunnar had raised the window before we went to sleep to air out the room, so I could hear the swish of the grass as it was parted by unseen legs. The whispering stopped. I wanted to look out the window to see who was there, but I stayed by the wall, frozen.

A light flickered across the room and snagged my attention. Poppie's easel faced the window, and on its frame hung a small round shaving mirror. In the mirror a reflected face sneered at me, moonlight washing over the features. I knew that face, the dark eyes and white hair, the sharp nose and chin. Once it had seemed achingly beautiful. But now it was sinister and very scary. It was Bog, the boy on the motorcycle. And somehow he had followed me to the farm.

He winked and I knew he could see me in the mirror as well. I must have looked pretty pathetic, clinging to the wall. Bog blew me a mocking kiss and the window fogged for an instant with his breath. Then he tapped lightly on the glass and I flinched.

Keeping my eyes on the mirror, I leaned down and gave Gunnar's leg a hard shake. "Gunnar," I whispered hoarsely. "Gunnar, wake up. Someone's out there."

Gunnar didn't budge.

"Anne, Gunnar," I tried again, this time more insistently, as Bog crooked a white finger toward me. "Wake up, you guys!"

But neither of them stirred.

Bog put his hand on the sash and started to push up the old window. I looked frantically for something to use as a weapon, and saw Poppie's hawthorn cane in an umbrella stand near the door. It seemed so far away, but I just couldn't meet Bog empty-handed. What did he want from me, coming here like this? Who was he? The window scraped in its weathered frame. A cool night breeze shivered against my sweating skin. I launched myself across the room, stumbling over Gunnar's outstretched legs to reach Poppie's cane.

I grabbed it in both hands and turned, swinging its solid weight over my shoulder like a club. One white hand clutched the inside of the sill. The other was pushing the window up higher. I moved closer to hit him. He was laughing, and as the full lips opened wide, I saw small, sharply filed teeth.

But a loud snarl stopped us both. Bog jerked away from the window and shouted, enraged, at something beyond the window that I couldn't see. It answered with another defiant snarl. The cane was heavy and my arms trembled as I struggled to hold it ready. Bog's face twisted with rage and I cried out, seeing it transform on the other side of the windowpane. The white profile stretched, transforming into a reptile, glittering eyes pushed to the sides of his temples where the hair draped like dried marsh grass. A long slick tongue spit out angry threats.

Bog fell away from the window, hands raised to meet an attacker, and I gasped as I saw the badger. At least, I thought it was the badger. He, too, was transformed, into a large creature standing upright on two legs, looming over the pale, coiling body of Bog and baring his sharp white teeth. Black-and-white fur cascaded over the badger man's back and he made powerful sweeping strikes with silver-clawed hands.

I couldn't move, but remained frozen by the sounds of their battle. They shouted words I couldn't understand and the hair lifted off my neck. They slammed into each other, locked in combat, and fell away from my sight. But I felt them through the floorboards, the room shuddering each time they collided against the battered sides of the house. They snarled, growled, and shouted. And then, abruptly, the motorcycle started up again, the roar of the engine drowning the badger's growls.

The single headlamp of the motorcycle blinded me and I squinted into the brightness, Poppie's cane still held aloft, waiting. The engine backfired and the wheels skidded over the gravel. The beam of light angled across the ceiling, then was gone. I was again in the dark studio, Anne and Gunnar sleeping soundly as if nothing had happened.

My arms ached. Stiffly I lowered the cane and looked about me. It was quiet, the darkness soft and calm, except for the terrified throb of my pulse. Anne turned in her sleep, her face settling deeper into the pillow. I was chilled and sweating, my breath rasping loudly. I stared dumbly at the cane in my hands, then walked to the window and looked out.

Nothing. Nothing but the stars shining over the tops of the trees. I collapsed on my bed again and tried to gather my scattered wits. What was happening here? To me, to Poppie, to the farm? Why did it seem we were all under attack?

I lay awake for a long time, trying to tease out of that one awful moment some kind of meaning. Had it been a nightmare? I had had vivid dreams before that lingered long after I had awoken. I turned restlessly on my bed. But all I could do to settle my fear was recall that I had not faced Bog alone. Someone, even if it was only a dream, had come at the last minute and fought for me. I made myself remember the badgerman, imagined him out there protecting me. He was still there, I told myself, walking Hannah's garden, guarding the house. *It'll be all right*, I told myself. *It'll be all right with him out there*. I relaxed a little, and finally the warmth of the blankets and the soft crackle of the wood in the stove lulled me back to sleep.

✦ chapter eight ✦

THE PHONE WAS RINGING. ON the couch, Anne groaned and put a pillow over her head. Gunnar muttered and half sat up in one of his two chairs. I rose groggily and went to find the phone.

"Where is it?" I yelled, hearing the ring but not being able to place it.

"The parlor," Anne mumbled from deep within her pillow.

I forded through the boxes in the hallway and stumbled into the parlor, which, if anything, looked more dismal than the night before. The phone was louder, but I still couldn't find it. I swore but uncovered the phone at last, hidden under a pile of newspapers, and grabbed it, convinced the caller would hang up the instant I answered.

"Hello?" I shouted.

"Hello. Is that you, Anne?" a man asked.

"It's her daughter, Cassie. Who's this?"

"Cass, it's me, Father Tom. Listen, I wanted to call as soon as I could. I stopped by the hospital early this morning and checked in on Daniel. It looks like he's doing better. He's had a good night anyway. But how are you guys? Are you doing all right out there? When

I heard you were at the farm I was worried."

"Yeah, we're all right, I guess. It's awful, but we're managing." I looked around at the ravaged parlor, both my anger and my fear returning. "It's going to take a lot to clean up this mess."

"You know I feel terrible about this," Father Tom said, and I heard his anxiety. "I needed to spend some time with my mother, who was not doing too well herself last fall. Melvin had offered to look in on Daniel from time to time, and since he's so close, I thought it would be a good plan. But after seeing the farm the other day, I don't know if I made the right decision. I wanted to say something to Anne."

"Do you think Melvin did this? Dumped all this stuff here?"

"Oh, I don't think so. He's a bit rough around the edges, but a good man, I think."

That doesn't say much for you, Father Tom, I thought bitterly.

"I'm just glad I found Daniel when I did. A friend of mine had stopped by to talk about the music for our church benefit dance. He's a well-known fiddler around here, very much in demand at these things. He happened to mention that he'd been walking in the woods and noticed that there was no smoke coming from the chimney. It was a cool morning and he thought that was odd. He asked me if the farm was vacant, as he had an interest in buying it."

As Father Tom talked, I thought of the gray-haired

fiddler from the Dubliner. The fiddler in Poppie's drawing.

"Anyway, I got worried and came out here myself to check on Daniel. When I saw him slumped over in the garden, I prayed I wasn't too late."

"He was lucky you were there to find him," I said honestly. "And I'm really glad to hear that he is doing better. I know he would be so much happier here on the farm. But I have no idea how we're going to clean this mess. There's just so much garbage everywhere." A shrew with dirty gray fur and a long snout climbed out of the gutted sofa and scurried under a box. I shuddered.

"Listen, the least I can do is give my brother-in-law Rob a call. He's got a pickup truck and would probably be willing to help you haul some of that stuff out of there for pretty cheap. Would tomorrow be soon enough?"

"Yeah, that's great. I'll tell my mother. And thanks for the good news about Poppie."

"You're welcome. And please, say hello to Anne for me, and tell her she can call me anytime."

"I will, thanks." It was good news to savor in that filthy room. Poppie was better and we had help coming to clean the farm.

"Hey, you guys!" I shouted. "Get up!" I crowed, bursting into the studio.

"What is it?" Anne asked, pushing back the blankets to sit up on the couch. She stretched her arms to the warming shafts of sunlight. She was as pale and delicate as the white camisole she wore.

At times like this I wondered how we could ever be related. How could I be so small and dark, like something dragged up from the bottom of a leaf pile in fall, while she seemed to have no more substance than light? She towered above me, a shaft of golden sunlight in which the white dust swirled and condensed into the luminous form of my mother.

"What is it?" she asked again, more urgently, frightened by my silence.

"That was Father Tom. Poppie's doing better."

"He is?" Her voice was husky.

"Yeah, he also said he'd call his brother-in-law to come and help us haul all the trash away tomorrow afternoon. Maybe we can get this place cleaned up before Poppie comes home."

"Oh, God, it never ends." Anne sighed and lay back on the couch, pulling the covers up again as if to protect herself against the messy task ahead. She stared at the ceiling, and her expression sharpened with resolve.

"Yes, all right. Let's clean," she said with conviction. "I smell coffee. Perfect." So that was where Gunnar had gone.

She dressed quickly, and twisted her golden hair into a braid. "Has anyone tried the john yet?" she asked me anxiously, tying her sneakers.

"Yeah," said Gunnar. He entered the studio carrying a small tray with toasted bread, cheese, apple slices, and three cups of steaming coffee.

"Well?" I asked, taking a piece of toast.

He shrugged. "Toilet works fine, just some rust in the water and bowl."

"No bats?" Anne asked.

Gunnar shook his head. "No bats; but don't sit on anything either."

Anne and I groaned.

"Well, some things you just can't get fussy about," she said. "I remember when it was only the outhouse . . ." Her voice trailed behind her from the hall. "Oh. Oh, God," she groaned. "This is so disgusting."

Gunnar gave me a wolfish grin. "You're next."

"I can hardly wait."

Anne returned, and gave me a little grimace. It was my turn.

The bathroom was much worse than Anne's cry of "disgusting." Bizarre black fungi were growing along the sides of the toilet in huge scalloped shelves. The bathtub, though filthy with scum, was still beautiful. It was long and deep and sat on brass clawed feet that, at the moment, were tarnished green. The crystal taps were opaque with dust. As a little girl, I had spent hours in here, floating like a captured mermaid while water sprites hovered in the rising steam. The wallpaper's dark green pattern of ferns was spotted with real moss and mold. I turned the taps on the pedestal sink and rusty water spat out from the faucets. I let it run until it was clear again, then washed my face and hands, drying them on my sweatshirt.

Anne and Gunnar were sitting at the kitchen table.

Anne's hands were wrapped around her coffee mug and Gunnar was seriously smoking a cigarette.

"So, where do we start?" I asked Anne.

"Believe it or not, I found some cleaning stuff in the pantry. I'll take the kitchen," Gunnar volunteered.

"He's the cook." Anne smiled at me.

"Let's do the parlor together," I said. "What about upstairs? Maybe our old room is okay?"

Anne shuddered. "I'm afraid of the bats."

"It's day," Gunnar said. "They're probably sleeping, if they came back here at all. I'll come with you to check it out."

"Please. You're taller than me, you'll make a better target." Anne laughed, but she twisted her braid.

We took the stairs slowly, Gunnar in the lead, then me, and Anne last of all. The top floor smelled musty, but the bats seemed to be gone. I heard the faint scritching of claws and raised my eyes to the leaves of dried paint peeling from the ceiling.

Gunnar pointed to a square hole in the ceiling of the hallway. "Does it lead to the attic?"

"Yeah," Anne replied. "There used to be a trapdoor but it's gone now. That must be how they got out last night."

"There's probably a second entrance from outside, under the eaves of the house," Gunnar ventured. "I'll nail something over it to keep them out."

We tackled the bedrooms next, and at each door I steeled myself against what awful thing we might find.

Two of the rooms turned out to be undisturbed. The beds were made, though dust had settled like a fleecy counterpane over the faded quilts. The old sepia photographs had almost completely faded away in their chipped gilded frames. Then Anne opened the door to the third room.

We stayed here every time we came back to the farm. It had once been Anne's bedroom, large and sunny with two windows that looked out over Hannah's garden. The pale yellow wallpaper had been torn off in long jagged pieces that exposed the cracked and rust-stained plaster beneath. The bed had been tipped over, its old wooden headboard smashed. The desk had been cleaved down the middle. It looked as if someone had used the room as a campsite. There were scorch marks on the floor, greasy soot around the windows, scattered bones and empty liquor bottles, painted symbols on the walls, and long, deep gouges in the wooden floor. The stuff in the dressers was strewn everywhere. I picked up a gingham dress, one of mine from years ago, out of a heap of jumbled clothing. It was stiff with mud and mildew.

"My things," Anne murmured sadly. "Our old clothes . . . my letters . . ."

Her face was ashen as she bent and retrieved something from a pile of dirt-speckled papers. It was a crumpled photograph of Poppie when he was much younger, well dressed in a baggy suit and a fedora hat. Standing next to him was a slim woman outfitted in a narrow two-piece suit and a small hat set at a jaunty angle on her blonde hair. She wore platform heels that showed off her well-shaped calves. Her lips were dark and full.

"Who's that?" Gunnar asked, pointing to the woman.

"Henriette. My mother," Anne answered.

"She was good-looking."

"She was hard," Anne said flatly.

I knew that tone. After all these years, she was still furious at her mother for running away and leaving her and Poppie.

We closed the door and retreated silently downstairs. I thought of Melvin Steiger camping out in my room. And, without warning, I thought about Bog, his creepy face rising through my memory. Last night might have only been a nightmare, but I couldn't shake the feeling that demons and trolls were invading our farm.

"Okay," Anne snapped, "let's get this crap out of here!" She threw open the front door and sunlight entered like the joyful return of a long-gone friend. Golden shafts chased up the wooden banister and buttered the stairs. They also lit up the dreadful collection of garbage and boxes. There certainly was a lot to throw out.

The morning air was sticky with the scent of the pines. I sucked in huge mouthfuls to clean the rank odor of the house from my nose and throat. A red-cheeked bird trilled from the top of a white pine, followed by the staccato rapping of a hidden woodpecker. I stood on the porch and saw a pair of deer amble along the edge of the woods, their sandy-colored hides dappled with sunlight. It was so beautiful here.

All morning Anne and I worked side by side, clearing out the boxes of junk, newspapers, and old bottles. We cursed the trash, cursed the weird molds on the walls and the critters that had made a home of our smashed furniture. I could hear Gunnar's Swedish and English cursing as he cleaned, hammered, and scrubbed in the kitchen. When the job in the parlor got too depressing, I took a break and went to look. He really *was* a Viking when it came to cleaning. All the cupboards were opened and scrubbed bare, except for the groceries we had brought with us. He had hammered back up a shelf in the old hutch and on it sat our few clean dishes. The bags of trash were gone. So, too, were the wormy mason jars that had contained gray-looking tomatoes. Of course, they might have been peaches. The grease was gone from the woodstove, and pots of water were steaming on its black cast-iron top. Even the refrigerator door was open. Gunnar was humming tunelessly as he sloshed bleach down its sides. His shirt was wet and dirty.

"Looks better, doesn't it?" he asked.

"Much! So what was in the fridge?"

"Don't ask."

"Animal, vegetable, or mineral?"

He thought for a moment. "All three." He grinned, and slapped some more bleach on the inside walls. "And you? How goes it?"

"It's better than it was, but a long way off from the way it used to be. Can you help us move out the couch? Anne doesn't think we can save it. It's pretty ratty."

Gunnar took a break and together we lifted the remains of the old couch. Lumbering under its weight, we took it out to the now-sizable trash heap on the driveway. A flock of sparrows had come inspecting, flitting over the mound as they searched the garbage. One flew off with the perforated edging from a piece of computer paper, and I guessed that a lot of the nests this year were going to look pretty spiffed up. The sun was bright, the sky a clear spring blue. The first honey bees buzzed in the opened heads of dandelions.

Reluctantly, I went back to the parlor and found Anne engrossed in a battered brown book.

"What is it?" I asked curiously.

"Hannah's journal. She kept one most of her life, you know." Anne sighed. "Poppie never let me read it."

"Where did you find it?"

"Hidden in the back of the sideboard drawer." She snapped the book shut before she handed it to me. "It's full of stuff about her garden. Have a look."

Amazed, I ran my hand over the smooth brown leather cover. I knew very little about my great-grandmother, just odd stories, Anne rolling her eyes to the ceiling every time she talked about her. But there had been pride in those stories as well. I opened the journal in the first half. The page was filled from margin to margin with smooth, elegant handwriting.

APRIL 6, 1913. Orville has gone ahead with his plan to purchase a farm in the cut-over land. We have heard from others that the Ben Faast Land Company is reputable, which is just as well since we are buying our farm sight unseen. Some of the farms in the cut-over turn out to be nothing but swamp, but Mr. Faast has assured us that with work, we should have a good farm out of the deal, with pastureland as well as two good fields. Orville leaves tomorrow by train to travel with the horses and all of our belongings. I am to take the passenger train and will wait for him in Ashland. I look forward to this adventure, though I am fearful for my delicate health. I am still not right in my body and pray nightly to God that I may be relieved of this sorrowful affliction. Orville believes that the move will change our luck.

I thumbed back a few entries to see if I could find out what she meant by her "affliction." I found another entry dated earlier, February 18, 1913.

Again I failed in my duty. I woke this morning to pain and blood. The child I had prayed for would not be held in my womb. Orville has been silent but I can see the terrible disappointment in his eyes. A man must have sons, a family to work the land. More than once I have been reminded that his mother brought forth thirteen children. He says my barrenness threatens to ruin us.

"What a life," I murmured to the beautiful handwriting. How many miscarriages did she blame herself for before she finally conceived Daniel? And then when she did have a child, a son no less, Orville left her anyway. No wonder she went a little crazy. But then again, maybe craziness was in the blood. Was that why her marriage had failed so miserably, and why Poppie's had failed as well? And all of Anne's relationships? I flipped forward, then gasped with astonishment.

"Awesome," I said to Anne. "Look at this."

Anne stopped sweeping and looked over my shoulder. There, spread out over two pages, was a sketch of Hannah's garden. I was seeing it as Hannah had first imagined it, before it was even planted and blooming. On paper the design looked bold and very ancient. The spiral path was broken by small stone areas that branched from the main stem of the path into lobed leaves, and scribbled over this were the names of plants, some scratched out and replaced by others as she sorted out her overall design. All along the margins were other drawings of plants in pen and ink, lightly shaded with watercolors. I recognized Poppie's artwork. I turned a few more pages and the drawings continued, giving shape to the words she had written.

"It's beautiful," Anne said softly. "They really understood each other, didn't they?"

A strange jealousy stole over me. It really was a collaboration. She listed the names of wildflowers, their properties to heal, and he drew sketches of them, their roots, their leaves and flowers. Occasionally Poppie's own humor surfaced and he transformed a wildflower into one of his little creatures. On one page the shaft of a dragonfly ended in a sword, while on another a sparrow had human arms and frog legs. His creatures were strange bits of his imagination, but they seemed at home here.

I closed the journal carefully, grateful that among all the destruction and trash, this treasure had been preserved, and set it on the sideboard, next to a stack of family photographs that Anne had salvaged and a packet of letters bound with a green ribbon. I looked at the stamps and saw the letters had come from France.

"She saved Poppie's letters," I said to Anne.

"Yes. At one time I think she saved everything that came her way. That was part of her culture. Keep a thing for seven years to see if you can find a new use for it."

"Was Poppie like that?" I asked, finding it difficult to imagine my grandfather aware of anything except the woods and his work.

Anne swept a pile of dirt into a paper bag, then stood, arching her back as she stretched. "Well, all of Hannah's things were very important to him. He kept them close to him all the time. But he never cleaned up or took care of them, either."

"But you did, right?" I said. She cocked her head and gave me a pinched smile. I knew this story. It was the reason Anne had an aversion to collecting stuff. Every time we had moved, she threw everything away and started over.

"That's right. I polished silver, even though no one came to tea. I dusted books, washed linens, and even sorted the pearl buttons in Hannah's sewing box—in addition to organizing Poppie's paintings, his receipts, opening his mail, and paying his bills. By the time I was twelve years old I was a great hand at forging his signature on checks." She shook her head. "A childhood spent as a curator in some weird museum. When I left I wanted to take nothing, own nothing, clean nothing . . . " She started laughing. Any excuse not to clean—our Finals pact, bad days, period days, full moons. I should have realized she was being messy on purpose.

"Was it all bad?" I asked.

She shrugged. "Was your childhood all bad?"

I was silent. It wasn't all that bad, but there were things that could have been better. Or at least different. I thought about Joe's family, their house filled at Christmas with relatives. Joe had never lived anywhere else besides that house. I didn't know what to say to Anne that wouldn't hurt.

"Hey, I did the best I could," Anne said defensively. "It really wasn't so bad, was it?"

"We moved too much. I couldn't make friends."

"I was buried here and no friends came to see me."

"I had no father."

"I had no mother," she countered.

I knew this game. Who was more miserable? Who had had the tougher life? She wanted me to be all right with how we lived, to admit to liking being the one who took care of her when things got hard, because she had suffered more than me. But I wasn't, and I didn't.

So I finally said what I had always thought. "You raised me to be your mother."

"Bullshit!"

"I paid the rent last month out of my savings when your school loan didn't show up on time. And the phone bill the month before, and the gas bill."

"And what about those damn violin lessons? Who pays for those?" she yelled.

"I earned those lessons, damn it! And I've been paying you back from my gigs ever since I was fourteen."

Gunnar came from the kitchen and stood looking perplexed at the pair of us facing off like angry cats.

"You're a kid. You don't understand anything about my life."

"Who does?" I cried, frustrated, swinging my arms wide to include the devastated parlor. "For once, explain it to me."

Anne glared at me, her face white, her lips pressed into a bloodless line. She was breathing hard and her hands were balled into fists. Slowly, she opened her hands and exhaled.

"You know enough. Hannah was crazy, Henriette was a cold bitch, and Poppie . . . " She paused, collecting herself. "Well, he never knew I existed except to keep his house. He only talked to Hannah, to the damn trees, and it took everything I had not to grow up into a loony like them. I *had* to leave." Anne looked around the room, helpless. "The worst part was I loved them." My mother's green eyes pierced me where I stood glowering. "I'm not a perfect mother, I know. But at least I tried. I left here to find a better life for you as well as for me. I don't want to sell the farm, but I believe that if I keep it, I'll lose my marbles and wind up back here, like them, alone and talking to trees."

Her face crumpled. Gunnar came close and put his arm around her. He looked at me with a mixture of sympathy and annoyance. He pulled her into the hallway and I heard her sobs echoing on the front porch.

I felt like such a toad. But it wasn't fair. Didn't I have a right to be angry? She may have been buried out here on the farm, but I got dragged all over the country as she ran searching for her new life. The only solid thing I had was this place and she wanted to get rid of it because she hated the memories. What I wanted really didn't matter, I thought angrily. So why did I feel so bad when I made her cry?

I needed to get some air. I grabbed Hannah's journal to take with me and a photograph fell out from between the pages. I picked it up and saw by the inscription that it was a picture of Poppie's baptismal celebration. An older priest sat at the table before a pile of uncut cakes, with all the good china and silver neatly laid out on a crocheted tablecloth. Beside him sat two other women in linen dresses and white lace collars. One woman held the teapot; both were smiling. Orville Brittman stood proudly by the sideboard, a big cigar in the corner of his mouth. His high starched collar looked uncomfortably tight. The other two men, farmers by the rugged look of their faces, flanked him.

I stared at young Hannah, her dark hair piled high on her head, holding baby Daniel, his white christening gown draped over her knees. I had only seen pictures of her as an elderly woman, and she was heavy and gray and always just out of focus. But here she was, and I touched the image, surprised to discover how similar we looked. Her head was turned slightly and she was looking off to the side at someone else in the photograph.

Right at the edge, almost out of the frame, I saw the fiddler sitting on a chair by the window. The fiddle with a woman's head scroll rested on his knees and his eyes were on Hannah. The same gray hair, the same long face. Trembling, I slipped the photograph back between the pages.

I swayed dizzily, as if caught in a whirling trap. The walls of the parlor expanded and the floor rolled in little waves. A shadow slipped across the wall and something brushed my arm. The fine hair prickled as goose bumps stood up on my forearms. An idea grabbed my ear and whispered into it. *It's all the same fiddler, the fiddler in Hannah's photograph not looking a day younger than when Poppie had sketched him leaning against the trees some sixty years later, and not a day older when I met him at the Dubliner two nights ago. And Anne knew him, too, had recognized him at the diner even though she had denied it.* The air around me grew tense, hushed as though it waited for me to speak. Clutching Hannah's journal, I fled the parlor, groped my way down the hallway through the kitchen and out into the sunlight of the garden.

Once outside, I gulped in mouthfuls of fragrant forest air, rubbed my arms for warmth, and tried to get my bearings. My thoughts were too far-fetched, too much like something Poppie might utter under his breath.

I looked at the ground for assurances that the world was not spinning. The muddied earth was solid and real beneath my feet, the new grass spears of green. The sun was bright and hot as I walked slowly through Hannah's garden, the journal hugged tightly to my chest.

My steps became steadier as I followed the winding path. Though it was damaged, sections buried in mud and brambles, I realized I had Hannah's original drawings and I could follow the outlines of her design. Amid the deep tire ruts there were signs of stubborn survival: a sprig of yarrow lifted new fronds from a patch of dried stalks, and there were delicate flowers of blue and violet. Hannah's journal told me they were rue anemone, and the green sprouts of a new vine were a sweet tuber she called fairy spuds. A wild rose was setting new buds even though it wore the old hips like ruby earrings on the thorny stems. Even torn apart and trashed by trolls, the garden had insisted on beauty.

On impulse, I went back into the house and retrieved my violin from the studio. With Hannah's journal in one hand and the violin in the other, I returned to the garden. I set the journal on the grass at the beginning of the path. I tucked my violin under my chin and started to play, walking slowly along the curving path. My fingers found the "Meditations from Thaïs," a slow piece with long, sad, dense bowings and a lot of vibrato. I knew why I had picked it. It was as close as I could come to imitating the fiddler's piece that night in the Dubliner. As I played, the pines swayed, the yarrow fronds bobbed their flower heads in the scented breeze, and small birds called out from the branches. It was soothing, and the chilly fear that had seized me in the parlor thawed in the sunshine.

I was wrong, I decided. In a small town like this, why should it be so odd to find familiar faces in old photographs? Surely this was my fiddler's father, or some other relative. The unusual fiddle had probably been passed down from one generation to the next. I teased myself for being goofy. It had been too many things at once: the nightmare, my argument with Anne, and the reminders of all the craziness in our family. Not to mention the ugly things that had happened to our farm. I was just spooked.

When I reached the center of the garden, I stopped playing and lowered the violin. I looked and realized there was a lot of work that needed to be done here, too. I stowed my violin back in its case, and opened Hannah's journal to the page with the garden, set it on a rock to be my guide, and stripped off my sweatshirt.

I worked for at least two hours, sweating in the climbing sun. I cleared away old tires, rusting pipes, a bed frame, and the rotting stumps of two trees. I leveled the deep muddy ruts and raked smooth the gouges. I was ecstatic when I found the broken flagstones that marked the spiral path along the edge of the garden. Some of the stones were still missing, but after searching I found them nearly buried under a bramble bush that didn't belong in the garden. Following the design, I reconstructed the old path with its leaves and curling stems of white stone.

At the first branching, where three stones formed the shape of a leaf, I found the buried stone sculpture of a hare. The two tips of its perked ears had pointed out of the soil like tulip leaves. I dug it out and washed it off with well water. The granite hare, resembling the one that had spooked me on the way to Martha's house, challenged me with its bold stare.

"Looks like I'm being followed," I said to the stone face. I set it down again on the path by the first set of leaves and continued to make my way along the inward curve.

There were other treasures to be found in the garden: a tiny silver salt spoon, thick shards of blue crockery, the broken arm of a china doll, and the slab of an amber-colored geode. The last I slipped into my pocket to give to Anne later. When we were talking to each other again.

Most of all, I was surprised and thrilled by the flowers and plants that I uncovered. They were beautiful, delicate, and wild, each one with its own personality. I had learned about many of them from Poppie when I was little, a game we used to play. But I had forgotten quite a few and now turned to Hannah's journal to name and learn about them. Harbinger-of-spring had tiny white flowers poking through the dead leaves, ram's-head lady's slippers unfolded rust-and-white orchid blooms along a slender stalk. White-spiked foamflowers shared a space alongside the blue hepatica and the broad fuzzy leaves of comfrey. Deep in a bed of pine needles were the pearl-white stalks of Indian pipes, a fungus that grew in the likeness of alabaster flowers. I shook my head in wonder. My great-grandmother may have been crazy, but she had a keen sense of nature and the skill to create this amazing work of art out of a garden of wildflowers.

"Cassie?"

I looked up and saw Anne. She was waiting outside the spiral garden as if she needed an invitation to come further.

I smiled, relieved to see her. "I'm sorry, Anne. I really didn't mean to snap at you."

"Yeah, me too. I'm just a little freaked out by all this."

"Hey, come here and see this," I said, wanting to show her the Indian pipes that were blooming near the center of the garden.

She walked slowly down the path, one foot carefully placed in front of the other. She stopped at the stone hare.

"Where did you find him?" she asked, pointing with her shoe.

"He was buried up to his ears."

"Good thing, too," she mumbled. "Always did cause trouble, that one."

"What?" I asked.

"Oh, nothing." She shrugged it off. "Hannah used to complain about a gray hare that made free with the plants in her garden. Poppie carved this hare after she died and stuck it in here. As a kind of memorial, I guess." Anne squinted in the bright sun at me. "You're a lot like her, you know."

I balked, wondering whether that was a compliment or an insult.

"No, no, I mean that in a good way," Anne said hastily. "Seeing you putter here in the garden. Hannah would have liked that, though I don't know if she would have let you in here when she was alive."

"Why not?" I pulled out a black rubber hose that was choking a bunch of violets.

"Private space. Like Poppie's studio. They guarded that space as though it was sacred."

"How did she die?" I asked, suddenly realizing that I didn't know.

Anne looked up into the trees as though the answer were there. "Drowned, I think. It's a bit vague. She went walking at night and they think she slipped into the marsh. No body was ever recovered."

"So the grave at the church at Ashland . . ."

"Empty." Anne nodded. "What's that over there?" she said, changing the subject.

I followed her gaze and saw the black-and-white fur of the badger as he sulked beneath the bushes. The pointed face stared back at us with a look of irritation. I smiled. "A badger. I think he has a burrow over by the well. We're probably disturbing his usual route home by being in the garden."

"Then maybe we should leave him in peace. Let's go and see Poppie. I called the hospital and they said the doctor should be there this afternoon."

"All right," I said, and reluctantly closed Hannah's

journal. I gathered up my violin and, as an afterthought, plucked a small handful of heartsease out of the swaying grasses. I wound the tall grass into a little wreath and hung it on my wrist.

"I suppose every animal in the north woods will be in our garbage dump tonight," Anne said, eyeing the squirrels scurrying into the trees with stolen slices of rock-hard bread.

"Yep. Word's gone out already. Free smorgasbord over at Brittman's place."

"It's the bears I worry about. They can be nasty this early in the spring."

"Do you think we should say anything to Melvin Steiger?"

"You mean like 'Get the hell out of here'?" Anne snorted in disgust. "Let's hope the creep has crawled back under his rock."

"So you think he's a creep, too?" I asked. "No one else seems to. It's almost like we're the only ones who find him repulsive."

"Hmm," Anne said absently, and chewed on her lip. "Maybe," she mumbled, and turned back toward the house.

I glanced over my shoulder at the garden before going in and grinned, seeing the badger stroll through the winding paths. He buried his face in the violets, scratched at the bare earth a little, and disappeared down a hole in a grassy knoll beside the well.

⋆ chapter nine ⋆

BY THE TIME WE HAD reached the hospital, the sun was trailing long afternoon shadows behind the trees. We pulled into the little parking lot and I saw Melvin's black pickup truck, its left fender badly dented, the right one tied on with a rope. Ribs of scrap wood had been slapped up as sides. In the flatbed there were gnarled tree stumps, their fleshy roots dangling over the edge. The broken branches with their leaves and withered berries told me they were the remains of mountain ash, a tree my grandfather prized almost as much as the pines.

We walked past it and Anne bristled. Her boot heels hit the concrete hard as she strode across the lot. Gunnar and I exchanged a quick glance. I didn't know how well he knew Anne, but public rages were one of her specialties and one was developing right now. The etiquette guides of Miss Manners and Emily Post never interfered; she would shout, argue, and swear like a rocker at a heavy metal concert at her opponent, preferably in full view of a crowd. I still blush remembering the science teacher she had blasted at a parents' conference. I had to face him in class the next day and pretend I hadn't heard a thing about it.

This time, for once, I wasn't apprehensive. If Melvin was stupid enough to be here after what he had done to our farm, then he deserved a double blast from Anne's rage gun. I just hoped Gunnar could handle it.

Anne marched past the front desk, brushing off Nadine, whose hand was raised in greeting.

"Well, I never . . ." she complained. But it was too late. Anne had already grown impatient with the elevator and had started up the stairs. Gunnar and I had to run to catch up.

I was completely out of breath by the time we reached the fourth floor. Even Gunnar was huffing, taking the steps two at time. I saw Anne charging down the lime-green corridor, her fine blonde hair whips of straw.

"Wait!" I called to Anne, trying to rush my aching legs. "Wait. Let's go in together."

She turned to us, tapped her foot, and waited exactly ten seconds. Her face was shell white, her eyes livid green.

"Excuse me," called a nurse as Anne headed for Poppie's room. "Excuse me, but you can't go in there," the nurse tried again, rushing out from behind the desk to stop us.

"And why not?" Anne demanded, turning on the young woman.

At Anne's blazing face the nurse backed up a step. "This is ICU. Only immediate family is allowed."

"I'm Daniel Brittman's daughter."

"Oh," the nurse faltered. "I'm sorry. I didn't know. I thought your dad was alone. Except for Mr. Steiger. He's in there now with him."

Anne spun on her heel. Close at her side, feeling the heat of her rage, I followed her into Poppie's room.

Melvin was leaning over the steel railings of the bed, his mouth close to Poppie's ear, whispering. Poppie's eyes were wide with terror and his hands fluttered weakly over the sheets.

Anne grabbed Melvin by the collar and roughly jerked him backward. "Get away from him," she yelled. "Get away from all of us."

Melvin gagged as Anne's grip tightened, choking him. Then, twisting his body, he reached around to punch her. An IV stand rocked back and forth as Anne tried to avoid Melvin's fist. They struggled in the tight space between Poppie's bed and the nightstand. Frightened faces appeared in the corridor window and I could hear the rapid clatter of feet outside. A code dinged loudly over the speakers.

"Get away, you monster!" Anne was screaming. She had the advantage of height and surprise, slapping and scratching him with one hand while the other kept a firm grip on his collar. I stood there, stunned. Gunnar pushed past me and reached to pull Anne away. I saw it was a mistake the moment his hand was on her arm, restraining it.

"No! Gunnar, don't!" I shouted, lunging at Melvin. I was too late. Melvin's fist shot out and clipped Anne hard on the chin. Her head snapped back and she flailed backward into Gunnar's arms.

"Goddamn," Gunnar bellowed, and Anne crumpled to the floor at his feet.

By this time the security guards had arrived. A young guard shoved Gunnar against the wall, shouting at him to put his hands up and spread his feet. Anne curled on the floor, blood flowing over her chin. Melvin was hunched over, his face hidden behind his hands, swearing.

"That's enough," an older guard told him.

Melvin lifted his head. "She attacked me!" There were three bloody slashes across his cheek. The skin was blotched, white and muddy red with outrage.

"I want a restraining order! Get me a restraining order," Anne was demanding. "That creep doesn't belong in here!"

"I said be quiet, both of you!" the guard ordered. "This is a hospital. You've got no business brawling like a pair of drunks in here."

"That son of a bitch has no business in here at all," Anne snapped as she stood swaying at the foot of Poppie's bed. The gash on her chin was bleeding heavily.

"Look, we're gonna have to straighten this out some-where else. You and you"—he pointed to Melvin and Anne—"come with me. And somebody call a doc for her."

"What about this one?" the younger guard asked, motioning with his head to Gunnar, pinned against the wall.

"Bring him along," the guard said as he pushed Melvin through the door.

"You stay here," Anne said to me as they were led away. "Look after him."

Almost immediately, two nurses bustled in to check on Poppie.

"I think you should leave," one said coldly.

"I think not," I retorted, standing next to Poppie's bed. "This wouldn't have happened if you had followed *your own rules* of not allowing anyone but family into the ICU. My grandfather needs me. Needs to know I'm here. So I'm staying."

The two women looked at each other with irritation. But I was right. They had let that troll in and he had filled the room with his nasty self. The pungent stink of smoke and marsh still hung in the air. One nurse straightened the IV stand and replaced the bag. The second took Poppie's pulse.

I pulled up a chair and sat next to him, holding his other hand.

Despite the battle that had just been fought over him, he looked calmer, his eyes half closed like a child falling into sleep. Earlier, they had taken out the respirator and washed and shaved his face. A thin tube of oxygen looped over his ears and under his nostrils. His cheeks were gaunt, but beneath the pale skin, there was a faint pink hue that gave me hope. Despite his labored breathing, I knew he was getting better. I took the little wreath of heartsease off my wrist and placed it in his hand. As soon as the leaves touched his palm, his fingers closed over it. A surprised expression crossed his face. His eyelids opened slowly, the dark pupils a milk gray. They turned ever so slightly to find me.

"Hey, Poppie," I said. "It's me, Cassie."

His cracked lips parted to speak. He whispered something, his voice dry as an old leaf.

"What?" I asked, leaning closer. Even the nurses had stopped their fussing and were watching Poppie with interest.

"*Polygonum persicaria*," he repeated. He closed his eyes again and drew in a deep ragged breath.

"What did he say?" asked a nurse.

"He identified the plant in his hand," I told her. "He knew what it was by touch."

The nurses exchanged glances of bewilderment. Poppie must have seemed too doped up to them to even be aware of the heartsease in his hands. I was both relieved and a little disappointed. I had wanted him to be just as pleased to see me.

But I didn't want to give up. I took Genie's advice, and talked to Poppie as though he knew me, as though it were normal. I told him that Anne and I were at the farm. That we were cleaning away the garbage and that I was working in Hannah's garden. I told him about the badger and the Indian pipes. Though he seemed distant, his eyes drifting back and forth beneath the half-closed lids, I knew he heard me. Sometimes his gaze would settle on my face and he would smile. Only once did he say anything. I told him about finding the granite hare in the garden.

He chuckled dryly. "It's a costly tune he fiddles, but in the end it's worth the price," he rasped.

141

I stared confused, trying to figure out the meaning of his words. I knew that there had to be some connection but I didn't have a clue.

Anne and Gunnar showed up finally, a young resident trailing anxiously behind them. Anne looked like a triumphant warrior queen, her back erect, her shoulders squared for battle. There was a neat row of tiny stitches along her chin. Her eyes glittered proudly. Gunnar was more subdued, his hands shoved into the pockets of his jacket. He looked a little grim and uncertain. Worry lines creased his forehead.

"How's he doing?" Anne asked, coming beside me. Her voice was husky.

"Better," I answered. "He spoke to me."

"He did?" said the startled resident. "That's great. We weren't sure how well he was progressing. We thought there might be some permanent damage when he arrived here."

"My father is eccentric," Anne explained, "and not too many people understand him even when he's healthy. But he's tough." She looked around the cold, sterile hospital room. "And I don't think he would choose to die here."

"Well, I hope you're right," the resident replied. "But he does need to be here a bit longer. He could easily have a relapse."

Anne was quiet but her eyes found mine. *He needs to get out of here*, they said.

I agreed, but I didn't think any of us was ready for

that kind of responsibility yet. "We could use another day or so to finish cleaning up the farm," I whispered back.

She nodded, took my hand, and gave it a squeeze. Then she pulled a chair and sat beside Poppie, stroking his cheek and talking softly to him.

"What happened with the police?" I asked.

Anne shrugged. "I have a ticket."

"And Melvin?"

She shook her head and grimaced. "Talked his way out of it. He's got them all in his hand."

I glanced at Gunnar's weary face. If he was like the rest, not reading Melvin the way Anne and I saw him, this had to be weirder than weird for him. I felt a dart of sympathy. At least he was still here. "Gunnar, do you want to come with me to get something to drink? Maybe some coffee?"

"Yeah sure, why not?" he said. "Anne, do you want us to bring you back some tea?"

She smiled at him apologetically. "Some cake, too? Or maybe a candy bar?"

"We'll be back soon," I said, and left, ignoring the stares of the nurses. Downstairs in the cafeteria, Gunnar put three packets of sugar in his coffee and stirred it nervously. "I really want a cigarette, but you can't smoke anywhere around here."

"Come on, then, let's take a walk outside. It's depressing in here anyway," I said.

No sooner had we come through the glass doors than

Gunnar lit up a cigarette. He shook his head, his blond hair blowing in the evening breeze. In the neon lights of the hospital he looked haggard.

"Those'll kill you, you know," I said, pointing to the cigarette in his hands.

"Yeah, I know," he said, bowing his head. "I promised Anne I would quit. But now doesn't seem to be a good time."

We started down the street, just drifting quietly in the spring twilight. A few early stars winked between the tall branches of the elms that lined the sidewalk. The music of a fiddle wafted on the night wind, over from the festival. A drum sounded a heartbeat and my feet lightly marched in time to it. Somewhere in the city square, there were people dancing.

"Why does she do that?" Gunnar said, exhaling smoke.

I assumed he meant Anne's rage. "Contrary to what everyone thinks, Melvin is not a good guy. Take my word for it. He's responsible for the way things are at the farm, for Poppie's illness."

"No," he corrected me, "I'm not asking about what she did to Melvin. I think I understand that. And maybe she's right about the guy. He seemed nice enough. But the farm is a mess. No, what I don't understand is why she won't let me pay for anything. Not even the gas or the groceries on the way up here. You must think I am a stingy man. But I have tried, Cassie, to help her with money, honestly, and she always refuses. She always says everything is fine, she's doing great. And then I hear the two of you arguing about money. And you, her teenage daughter, having to pay the bills. Why can't she tell me the truth?"

Part of me thought I didn't really owe him any explanation. I could have just blown it off. But I hesitated. He'd put up with a lot. And he'd just taken her side in the fight with Melvin—even though he wasn't sure. I decided to be straight with him. "Pride," I answered. "And stubbornness. She's had a lot of boyfriends who just messed with her and left her in the lurch. They usually ask her for stuff, like 'Be my trophy girlfriend,' or 'Pay my phone bill,' or 'Hey, babe, got a couple of bucks until next week?' They haven't usually offered help, and maybe she's afraid there'll be a catch or something behind it."

"So she doesn't trust me?" Gunnar said flatly. He took another drag on his cigarette.

"I think she wants to, Gunnar. A lot. But she needs time to get used to the idea. I mean, look at this mess we're in, not just the farm, but her whole family. People left her all the time. Until me"—I grinned—"and I really didn't have a choice. My mom is so good at telling stories because that's how she survived as a kid. She made herself into a heroine of some fantastic fairy tale just because she needed to know that it was possible to survive her family situation."

"How did you come to be so wise, Cassie?" he asked me gently.

I laughed, a little embarrassed. "Not all that wise. I just know her. And I love her, even when we fight. She's such an irritating combination of things, smart, funny, caring, and then irresponsible, sloppy, and bitchy." I burst out laughing. "I sound like I'm describing my kid, not my mother, don't I?"

Gunnar laughed with me and laid a hand over my shoulder. "If Anne isn't ready yet, at least let me help you, Cassie. Maybe together we can let Anne be that heroine. After what's just happened, I know she's certainly not afraid to face the devil head-on."

Standing there on an Ashland sidewalk in the twilight, I wanted to believe him. That he was the one who would be there for Anne.

"Okay, deal," I said, cautiously, happy that for once I had an ally.

We were standing in front of a small grocery store, a couple of red-and-white signs proclaiming that it carried tasty homemade sausages. Through the window, I could just make out the black-and-silver rectangle of a phone box. Suddenly, I really wanted to hear Joe's voice.

"You know, I want to make a quick call to a friend," I said to Gunnar, pointing to the phone. "Let him know what's going on."

"Sure," he answered, and stubbed out his cigarette. "I wanted to get new fuses for the farm."

I quickly wound my way through the congested aisles to the phone at the back of the store. It was tucked at the end of the housewares section, nearly hidden by bright orange-and-blue boxes of detergent. Around the phone on a spare piece of wall were scratched various numbers followed by all sorts of obscene promises. A few crude drawings were included for those whose reading skills might not have been up to the task. The receiver felt sticky, the faint odor of cheap cologne lingering on the mouthpiece. I punched in Joe's number and then our calling card number and waited. The phone lines stuttered and clicked, a mechanical operator thanked me, then it started ringing. I squeezed the phone tightly in anticipation.

"Hey, baby," a man crooned.

But it wasn't Joe, for the phone was still ringing somewhere far away.

I looked up and saw Bog leaning against the detergents. His heavy leather jacket hung open and in the bright light he was the color of chalk, his skin like milk poured over a frame of bones. A nasty gash raked his white throat, a red smear above the shivering leaves of his tattoo. His eyes were dark, a thin green rim circling the opaque pupils. He worked his lips into a kiss and sucked noisily on his teeth.

The ringing stopped abruptly and very far away a voice said, "Hello?"

I hung up the receiver without uttering a word.

"Who the hell are you?" I whispered, my hand still resting on the receiver.

The fine nostrils flared and he opened his eyes wider. "Why don't you come here and I'll show you?" He tucked his thumb into the waistband of his jeans, the long white fingers outlining his crotch. He stepped toward me, his hips leading. He whistled softly a tune that snared my head in a thin string of piercing sound.

"Go away," I said thickly. But the dark eyes were inviting, the white hand on his hip dazzling. Just beneath my ribs my heart beat in fear and something else—anticipation, excitement. Sudden feelings of longing and desire swept over me like a wave. He kept whistling and the tune was a net, and though I flinched against the tugging strands, I also wanted to go to him. The garish boxes of detergent faded as I saw only his pale face, his full lips. He leaned down, face close to mine, his silky long hair enclosing us like a pale tent. His hand reached for mine. I gasped at the stinging coldness of his fingers. I thought of Joe, warnings screaming far and away in the back of my head, but it wasn't enough. I raised my face to the kiss that was coming.

"There'll be no wall between us tonight," he whispered. "I've seen to that."

Pressed close to him, I could smell the musty odor of his body. His eyes glittered, his black pupils were slits.

"Go away," I said weakly.

His fingers curled around mine. He bent my wrist back and pressed down. My knees buckled.

"Oh, no, baby. You're mine."

"Cassie," Gunnar called out. "Cassie?"

The cold hand released me instantly and I slowly straightened.

Gunnar rounded the corner, a bag of groceries in one arm. "Did you make your call?"

I didn't answer. My freed hand throbbed with cold. Bewildered, I turned back to the boxes of detergents, but Bog was gone.

"Is everything all right?" Gunnar asked, coming closer. "Your face is all flushed. Did you hurt your hand?"

"I'm fine," I stammered. I glanced down and saw that I was cradling my hand as though it had been wounded. My skin was dead white where Bog's fingers had gripped my wrist. I tried to rub the warmth back into the frozen skin.

"Did you talk to your friend?"

"No one home," I lied.

"Well, we should get back," Gunnar said. "I'm a little worried about leaving Anne and your grandfather too long."

"Yeah, she'll be needing her cake about now," I said with a weak smile. The narrow aisle of the grocery store was spinning out of balance, and I felt the same vertigo I had had in the parlor. Time had shifted and nothing felt real or solid. For a moment I believed I could simply walk through the boxes of detergents and into the street. I tried to remember what I said to Bog. Why had I hung up on Joe? Why was my hand so cold?

"Then let's see if we can coax her out of the hospital and go to a restaurant," Gunnar said, leading the way out of the store. "The cake in there looks pretty awful. And besides, I want a hamburger. And a beer."

"Yeah, me too," I added without thinking, watching the street, wanting and not wanting to catch sight of Bog.

"Ask your mother about that," he said with a chuckle.

"Oh, no. I just meant I want something to eat," I said, flustered. I licked my lips. They felt dry. Why was my heart beating so fast?

"Cassie, are you sure you're all right?" Gunnar stopped and peered closely at my face.

I backed away, absurdly afraid he would see the image of Bog still reflected in my eyes. "No, really, I'm fine," I said. "Really." I smiled thinly.

We picked up our pace and hurried back to the hospital. The sound of a fiddle followed me, its tune merry and brisk. The ground beneath my feet grew more solid, the night air refreshing. I opened my ice-cold hand and imagined catching the notes as they fell like warm rain in my upturned palm.

⋆ chapter ten ⋆

IT TOOK GUNNAR AND ME a while to convince Anne to leave Poppie and come out to dinner.

"You need the break, Anne," Gunnar said firmly. At last she relented and, with a heavy sigh, relinquished Poppie's hand.

We found a little bar and grill not too far from the hospital. Except for an ugly green lamp hanging over the pool table, it was dimly lit and almost cozy. We sat down in a round corner booth with plump leatherette seats. A jukebox crooned out a country tune, and two men playing pool ogled Anne briefly before returning their attention to the colored balls scattered over the green table. We ordered hamburgers, fries, and salad. Anne and Gunnar washed theirs down with a pitcher of beer while I had a chocolate shake. Gunnar finished off his meal with coffee, which he complained was only brown water, and a piece of gooey-looking apple pie. Anne had German chocolate cake.

None of us said much during dinner. We all seemed to chew over our private thoughts as much as the meal. Gunnar held Anne's hand, though his worried eyes looked down at his coffee. Anne stared off over the bar into a place I couldn't see. And I was no less distracted. I didn't know how to tell Anne and Gunnar about Bog. I wanted to very much. I knew he was dangerous. I knew this was a bad thing. But every time I tried to summon his name, to speak it out loud, I couldn't. It curled on the roof of my mouth and just stayed there. And there was something I didn't want to admit out loud. I was afraid, but I also wanted to see him again. *I had wanted that kiss*, I realized, perplexed by my own strange emotions. No, I thought firmly, wiping away the image of Bog and me, lips locked. That was crazy. *Get a grip, Cassie*, I ordered myself.

When the waitress brought the bill, Anne ordered a brownie and wrapped it in a napkin.

"For later," she said.

A brownie in her purse, that was Anne's security blanket. What was mine? I wondered, thinking I could use something solid to hold on to right now. The badger man of my dreams, I decided. He'd protect me.

While I distracted Anne, Gunnar went and paid the bill before she could object. Then we went to see Poppie one more time before leaving for the farm. Visiting hours were over in the hospital and a cleaning man was washing the floors on the fourth floor. The ICU was quiet except for the continual hum and beeping of machines. The lights in Poppie's room had been dimmed and he seemed to float in the green shade. His long white hands rested comfortably on the surface of the blanket, the little wreath of heartsease still wrapped in his fingers. I saw the nurse try to remove it, thinking him asleep. His fingers closed reflexively and he refused to give up the wreath.

"Let him keep it," Anne said to the nurse.

Anne's reputation must have preceded her to the night shift, for when the nurse spoke she was very careful choosing her words. "It's really not appropriate for him to have this here in the ICU."

"It's this room that's not appropriate for my father," Anne said sternly. "Let him keep the wreath."

Reluctantly, the nurse withdrew. She would probably try again, after we had left, but I didn't think she was going to have any better luck.

Anne took his hand and stroked the bruised inside of his arm. He opened his heavy-lidded eyes.

"Home," he said in a cracked voice. He turned his head stiffly toward Anne and pain furrowed his smooth brow. "Take me home."

"Soon," Anne whispered.

He moaned and his eyes settled on me. "I will pay the fiddler. I will pay the fiddler for us all," he said. His breathing grew rough, his chest heaving with the effort of speaking.

Scared, I laid my face close to his on the pillow. "I'll tell him," I said to reassure him. "Don't worry, I'll tell the fiddler." I didn't know what I was saying to Poppie, just guessing at what he needed to hear. It worked. He became calm again, and released his grip on Anne's hand.

The nurse hovered at the door. Somewhere behind the desk Poppie's panicked breathing had set off warnings on the machines. This time, when she asked us to leave, we did so without argument.

On the drive to the farm I lay down in the back seat of the Saab, stared out the window, and marveled at the complete blackness of the country roads. Not like the city, where the night sky is dusty with the glare of street-lights. Here the stars blazed blue, pink, and even green across the deep blue velvet sky, and a three-quarter moon lifted out of the crown of treetops. The heavy food we had eaten and the murmuring of the car engine made me sleepy. Gunnar had turned on the radio and I could hear an orchestra playing something romantic and light. I only roused myself when I felt the road change from blacktop to the rough gravel of our farm road. The car slowed and I sat up, rubbing my sleepy face. And then I was jolted awake as the Saab's headlights landed on our enormous garbage pile.

I had almost forgotten just how much trash and junk we had hauled out. But there it was, looking like a trash barge run aground in the middle of our yard. Little dark shapes flowed over the pile and in and out of its crevices. Scavengers had come to browse and snuffle through the boxes and bags. They had dragged bits and pieces all over the place, making the pile seem like it was growing. The headlights of the car picked out the green glare of raccoon eyes and then the bright yellow glow of a fox's stare. Crows strutted over the broken limbs of a chair, flapping their wings and cawing loudly. The raccoons scampered away from the pile, but not too far away, for I could hear them barking angrily at our intrusion.

"Yuck, what a mess. I almost forgot," I groaned.

"At least the bears haven't come out yet," Anne grumbled.

"It won't be here for long," Gunnar said, trying to cheer us up. "The guy comes tomorrow with the truck, right?"

"Yeah, but how many visitors do you think we're going to have tonight?" I asked as two sparrows tussled over possession of some couch stuffing. The long pink snout of an opossum peered out from a box, along with the little noses of her brood clinging to her back.

We left the car, aware of all the eyes that followed us. As I approached the house, I noticed a thin black trail painted down the porch stairs and congealed into a black puddle in the dirt path. I slowed my steps, wondering what it was.

"Careful," I warned Anne behind. "Something's all over the steps and path."

Nervously I walked up the stairs, sidestepping the trail that led to the front door. Then I stopped and a sickening coldness seized me.

"Oh, no," I breathed.

The door was open, swinging inward into the dark throat of the hallway. There was something long and bulky hanging on it.

Trembling, I reached for the doorknob and pulled it toward me. Moonlight spilled over the torn carcass nailed upside down to our door. An animal's battered head dangled toward the floor, the blood dripping with a steady *tick-tack* sound.

"Oh, my God," Anne cried, and covered her mouth. She backed away from the door and into Gunnar, who was coming up the stairs.

"What is it?" Gunnar asked.

"A badger," I said thickly. "Someone killed it and nailed it to the door."

"That bastard Melvin," Anne spat. "I'll kill him myself if I see him again."

Not Melvin, I thought, *but Bog*, recalling the gash on his throat. He had returned to the farm and murdered my protector. He was coming for me. A dank wind gusted out of the open door of our house.

"If Melvin did this, then he's much more dangerous than we thought," Gunnar said, concerned. "Perhaps we should sleep in a motel tonight."

"No!" Anne said.

"Be reasonable, Anne. You're endangering your life and that of your daughter."

"I won't leave. And I know how to protect myself here," Anne said sharply. "This is my farm."

"At least call the police."

Anne laughed. "So they can give me another ticket for hunting badger out of season? Melvin is playing them. Look, Gunnar, I know this is hard for you to believe, but I can handle it. If you want to leave, I'll understand. But I'm not going anywhere. If I let him scare me off now, neither I nor Cassie will ever be safe. There are dangerous things in the world. Sometimes you have to face them."

Yes. There are, I thought quietly, feeling again the icy chill of Bog's fingers on my wrist. And I knew with a cold certainty that my dream the night before had been real, as real as the bloodied corpse hanging on our door.

"This doesn't make any sense to me. But I am not going to leave you alone," Gunnar said, not too happily. "I'll fix the fuses so we can get some lights on here."

"I'll do that," Anne said. "I know where they are. And they've always been touchy. Can you please take care of this?" she asked Gunnar, looking at the badger.

"I will," I offered. I was heavy with sadness and fear. But I couldn't speak to anyone about how guilty I felt, how ashamed of my own conflicted desires for Bog.

It took a while, but Gunnar and I succeeded in pulling out the wooden stakes that had been driven through the badger's body. It fell in a messy heap, the head tilted upward so that the moonlight filled the empty black eyes. My stomach heaved as we rolled the corpse into newspapers and then into a large plastic bag. I got a shovel while Gunnar dragged the body to the well, near the grassy knoll that had been its home.

"Can you do it?" he asked. "I'll go help Anne."

"Yeah," I answered, and jammed the shovel into the soft soil. Gunnar left and all around me in the pines I could hear the muffled sounds of crying. I looked up but saw nothing. Then a mourning dove fluttered down from the branches of a white pine, its wings spread wide to catch the moonlight. It landed on the head of the stone hare and continued its mournful cries. Tears ran down my face as I dug the grave.

I placed the badger's body into the earth and filled in the hole. As I was finishing, smoothing the mound with the back of the shovel, lights popped on in the house. A bright incandescent glow flooded through the kitchen windows. The dove was startled and, lifting her wings, returned to the sheltered covering of the woods. I laid the shovel down and went around to the front of the house.

A naked yellow bulb burned from the ceiling of the empty parlor and a scattering of moths batted the glass windows with their urgent wings. The porch light illuminated the blood-splattered door and steps. My stomach churned and I turned away. It was more than I could do to clean that tonight. Anne cranked opened the parlor window and shouted out to me.

"Can you bring my brownie? I left it in the car."

"Yeah, I'll get it," I called back. I found it, wrapped in the napkin, sitting on the dashboard. I held it in my palm, testing its weight, wishing that it could offer me the same comfort it seemed to give Anne. I returned to the house, sensing the ever-watchful stares of the scavengers on the garbage pile, avoided the front door, and went along the side of the house to the kitchen. My sneakers grew wet in the deep grass.

As I rounded the corner, Anne leaned out the back door and set a bowl down on the back steps. She didn't see me. After she had gone back in, I saw that she had left out a bowl of milk. Next to it was the disk etched with the running hares. I saw her inside, tying some of the sprigs of dried herbs from the studio onto the window latches. She was whispering to herself as she moved from window to window.

I looked again at the bowl of milk, puzzled, until an old memory returned. I was three years old and we had returned to the farm after living in a big city that had made Anne cry a lot at night. She and I were standing on the stoop in summer. Fireflies were flickering in the bushes. I was holding a bowl of milk and it was heavy. Anne was telling me to set it down on the stoop and be careful not to get dirt in it.

"Who is it for?" I had asked.

"Wood folk."

"What wood folk?"

"Fairies."

My eyes had shone with excitement. "Will we see them?"

"No. They don't like to be seen, especially by sleepy little girls. Come inside, Cassie, and I'll tell you a story about them." She had nudged me to the door. I went with her, but glanced back, hoping to catch a glimpse of the wood folk drinking milk. That was Anne, never missing an opportunity to make her stories seem so real to me. It was probably a feral cat she had been feeding. But I remember being thrilled the next morning when the milk was gone.

"They came," I told her solemnly.

"Yes, they did," she had answered with a straight face.

"And did they dance, like you said in the story?"

"Go down to the field, Cassie, and look for the ring of mushrooms. That's their footsteps. Go look for yourself," she urged, and I ran into the tall grass, bright with excitement.

But now, as I waited on the kitchen steps, staring down at the white circle of milk in the bowl, I had other thoughts. Bog and the badger man. The ageless fiddler, Melvin reeking of wood smoke and something darker. Even the muddy knots that had been tied into my hair. Perhaps Anne had told me the truth when I was three and was willing to believe it, no questions asked. The truth as she had learned it from Hannah and Poppie. Anne feared something about the farm, enough to want to sell it. But she was also willing to fight for it, to leave milk on the back stoop and charms in the windows for the wood folk as a plea for their protection. And at that moment, confused, sad, and dreading the night, I wanted the same reassurance.

I gazed out over Hannah's garden, the patches of newly dug earth speckled with the lace of moonlight. My eyes filled, and the moonlight wavered over everything. Then, I caught my breath as from the center of Hannah's garden a transparent figure, bathed in a glowing light, emerged out of the tall fronds of a yarrow plant. Long, slender arms moved gracefully as the rippling figure followed the circular stone walk and then came to rest on a leaf-shaped stone.

A second figure stepped from the curtain of light and

followed the first, drifting easily along the widening curve of the garden path. Then a third figure shimmered to life, and a fourth. Arms outstretched, they joined to form a single band of shifting pale green light that undulated in a spiral over the garden, out to its edges.

The farther from the center they traveled, the more defined their shapes became. They looked like women dressed in long robes that parted as they moved, showing the curves of their breasts and rounded hips. A bell chimed and more colors swirled through them; blue, then orange and yellow, like polished gems. They didn't have faces, or at least not human faces. Perhaps they wore masks made of leaves and edged in thorns and flowers. They turned toward me and their eyes gleamed a soft gold. They tipped their heavy, leafy heads in acknowledgment. I stared at them in wonder. They turned and continued on without haste until they left the path of Hannah's garden and trailed through the long grass toward the pines. They paused briefly beside the lightning-scarred remains of two old white pines at the entrance to the woods.

Beneath the dappled shadows of the trees they bowed their heads in a salute, and as they straightened again, they transformed. Horns sprouted out of the leaves of the masks and their necks stretched into bright arches of brilliant light. Arms reaching, they fell forward and became white deer. And as I watched, spelled by the sight, they bounded away into the woods, streaks of lightning spearing the dark.

At my ankles I heard the soft lapping of a tongue in the bowl of milk. I didn't dare look down. Something brushed against my shin, neither furry nor leathery but a mixture of both. A tiny hand with a rough palm and twiglike fingers gripped my ankle as if holding on for balance.

And then I heard the fiddle. It was soft but insistent, as if coming from a long way off through the trees. The sound grew louder, the bow chasing the lively tune before it, until the woods echoed and crackled with the gritty notes. Rosin dust swirled amber streaks in the moonlight. Across the grass streaked the hare, bounding over the grass, his body rising and falling as he leaped in time to the music. Beside me on the stairs feet tapped, and a low humming followed the wild voice of the fiddle. I longed to stay and listen all night, but I knew from Anne's stories that I could not as a mortal, unless invited. And even that was risky. One could join the fairy dance and disappear for a century. When the fingers on my ankle loosened, carefully, very carefully, I edged away from the bowl of milk and mounted the kitchen stairs.

As my hand closed around the knob of the kitchen door, the music abruptly stopped. I waited, shocked by the sudden silence. Then my shoulders sagged. I turned to look. It was dark and quiet across the yard. There was no sign of the ghostly deer, no sound save the gentle hiss of the wind shaking the pines. Had I imagined it all? I glanced at the bowl of milk. It was half empty, its pale surface flat and still. I shook the strangeness from my shoulders and went inside.

I heard Anne and Gunnar talking in low voices in the studio. As I went to join them, the flickering white shapes that had trailed across Hannah's garden clung to the edges of my vision like fading sparks from fireworks, the music of the fiddle as maddening in my ear as a mosquito whine. The vertigo had returned, and I put a hand up to the wall to steady myself as I staggered through the hallway—and the wall yielded to my touch. The hallway contracted and expanded as though the house was breathing, and the wood gave off a sweet, damp odor.

I stumbled over the threshold of the studio as the floorboards heaved beneath my feet.

Anne looked up sharply. "Are you all right?" she asked urgently, her eyes searching my face.

"Yeah," I replied. "Just really tired." Her face seemed to relax.

"We could all use the rest," Gunnar said, straightening the covers of the couch bed.

"I'm going to the parlor," I said.

"It's cold in there," Anne protested.

"I just want to practice my violin. With the mute on," I added quickly, seeing Anne's frown.

"Okay, but come back here when you're ready to sleep," she said firmly. "I fixed this room up for us."

"Yeah, sure," I said, and ducked out. I needed to sort things out for myself. The things I'd seen were beautiful and terrible: a badger in the form of a man, ghostly women rising from the heart of the garden, the tattered corpse staked to the door, and the white imprint of Bog's cold fingers on my wrist. I trembled with the clamoring of strange emotions. A desire for phantoms, for the aching sound of a haunted fiddle playing in the pines and a flute that took away my breath and will. And for Poppie, a frail, old man full of riddles I couldn't guess.

I took my violin case, blankets, and a candle into the parlor and snapped off the glaring overhead light. Then, using one of Gunnar's many matchbooks, I lit the candle and set it on the sideboard. The room was otherwise completely empty. Anne and I had cleared out everything: trash, broken furniture, and smashed glasses. The black fungi and powdery molds were gone from the walls, and around the windows the flowers of the old wallpaper had a soft glow in the candlelight. There was the light scent of dried oak and apples. The windows were bare, with none of the sprigs of herbs that Anne had hung throughout the kitchen and the studio.

I folded my blankets and sat down, the violin case across my lap. When I unlatched the clasps and opened the case, a pungent whiff of cigarette smoke greeted me. *That's what comes of playing in bars*, I thought, and sighed.

My violin was old and long ago had been shellacked to a very dark brown that had turned almost black with age. It had a nice balanced sound, rich in the bass, smooth across the treble strings, and bright, but not shrill, in the higher positions. Some violins get husky or sound like they have a cold. But not mine. I loved it because it was loud and fearless. No matter how I was feeling, when I played it sang out with a true voice, refusing to be silenced. I tapped the heavy rubber mute onto the bridge, apologizing to the instrument for shushing it, and started playing.

Just scales at first, arpeggios to warm up my fingers, then chromatic scales, thirds, sixths, and eighths. But I was off, my fingers hunting for the notes instead of knowing them, as I usually did. I got frustrated and tried something else, the sarabande from one of the partitas in B minor. Its dark, discordant tone accompanied my unsettled emotions, but it wasn't enough. My concentration strayed and the bow kept slipping on the strings.

Silly girl, I thought, realizing I had forgotten to rosin my bow. I reached into the velvet case and found the small cube of rosin that the fiddler had given me. I held it up to the candlelight, watching the flecks of gold sparkle in the thick honey. I stroked it across the taut horsehair, almost mesmerized.

A wind stirred in the room from a broken windowpane, and the candle flickered. I didn't look up, but kept my eyes fixed on the flat band of horsehair I was rosining. Something had entered the room, whistling.

A wet, rank smell like the swamps in summer invaded on the breath of the wind. From the corner of my eye, I watched as the cool air condensed into a misty cloud, shrouding the walls of the parlor. The flower wallpaper wept. The hardwood floors, dry a moment ago, became damp and shiny as dew beaded up on the planks. I glanced sideways along the floor and beneath the window frame watched the black fungi return, pushing out through the walls. Water seeped along the moldings of the floorboards and brown stains fanned upward, peeling wallpaper and cracking the wet plaster.

My hand closed tightly around the fiddler's rosin. My movements were slow and deliberate as I skated it over the surface of the bow. I waited with dreamy calm. I knew what was coming. The tune grew stronger and I felt it like a noose around my neck.

"Hey, baby, it's me," a voice crooned softly. "Just like I told you."

I didn't know how Bog had entered the room. The window was still closed, as was the door to the parlor. But he was here, standing in front of me. I raised my eyes from the bow slowly. I saw his feet first. They were bare and covered with black mud, planted at the end of a dirty trail of mud and marsh grass that led to the closed window. Water sluiced down the broken pane and formed a trickling waterfall beneath the closed sill. A black wasp hovered above a spreading puddle on the floor.

My gaze moved upward. The legs of Bog's jeans were completely wet, as though he'd been swimming. The mud-streaked black fabric clung to the outline of his limbs. Red-capped lichens spread out along the seams and cuffs. Small snails slid on the side of one thigh. And still my eyes traveled upward slowly, taking in the increasing strangeness of Bog one moment at a time.

"Who are you?" I asked, my eyes no higher than his chest. He wore no shirt, and his white torso rose out of the black mud-covered jeans. My gaze lingered over the blue tattoos, spiral designs like the one painted on the wall upstairs. On his bare chest, I saw that the vine tattoo circled his torso from his waist to his neck, rising like mistletoe strangling an oak. "*What* are you?" I asked.

"Kin," he snickered.

My eyes jerked upward, and there, deep within the shining whiteness of his sculpted face, the eyes shone jet black. On his head he wore a tangled crown of nightshade. His white hair fell in glossy straight locks, draped over his shoulders like wet silk. The high cheekbones jutted in twin curves on either side of his long narrow face. His lips were full and blushed red as cranberries, the corners pulled into a sneer.

Handsome, almost handsome, I thought shivering, *if it weren't for his eyes.* They glistened, the color of wet rotting wood threaded with spirals of moss. I stumbled headlong into the well of those dark eyes as if falling into the tamarack swamps. The mist in the room thickened into a pool of water and the walls of the parlor disappeared. The glowing candlelight flamed green and then greener still as I saw the fragile leaves of duckweed and the tangled roots of fallen trees close over my head. I held my breath and thrashed, terrified, as I sank underwater, the green light fading into a murky brown.

"Take my hand," Bog whispered. "This house, these

walls are mere illusion. A door that opens to my world, where this night with me you shall go. Kin and blood-maiden. The pact will be made with the Red Clan once more."

Blindly I reached up and gasped as he took my hand in his icy-cold fingers. A shudder ran through me and I tried to pull away. But he held me tightly, and I could see the white moon of his face floating above me in the dark water. He bent down and his pale cheek brushed mine. His lips seared the hollow of my throat with a burning cold.

"No," I whimpered, and tiny bubbles drifted by my face.

Bog closed his mouth over mine to silence me.

The kiss was sharp, the taste of mud. He bit my lip, drawing blood. I struggled weakly against him. His mouth seemed to suck the last of the air out of my lungs. Then he released me, a cold hand circling my throat. He dragged me to the surface, and as my chin broke the stagnant surface of the water, I gulped a ragged, desperate breath of air.

"We're going now," he murmured, leering at my helplessness.

"The hell you are," shouted an angry voice.

His grip weakened for an instant and I took my chance, gasping at air, struggling wildly to free myself.

"Leave her alone," the voice commanded. "You can't have her, too!"

"She's mine already," answered Bog, gloating.

"Never!"

His cold hand shoved me fiercely under the surface of the water. It was dark and I was sinking, being pulled downward by the clinging arms of long-stemmed grasses and rotted branches. I opened my mouth and swallowed mud and weeds. Heavy, I sank into the silted bottom of a bog. I closed my eyes, folded my legs to my chest, and heard my pulse pounding like a slowing drumbeat in my ears. My lungs burned for air, but I didn't want to breathe anymore.

Dimly, I heard a splash far above me, and felt the water move as someone reached into the darkness and hauled me up. I was pulled through the muddy water to the surface. The hands that touched my face were warm.

"Cassie, Cassie, wake up!" the voice called urgently.

From behind the closed sheath of my eyelids there shone a golden light. I remembered the parlor and the candle. But as I opened my eyes I saw it was Anne. She blazed with fire, with heat and light. I opened my mouth to speak and coughed up mud and filthy water. My throat burned, my chest heaving as I remembered to breathe air.

"Fight back," Anne shouted at me.

And I became aware of a cold manacle around my ankle. I looked down and saw Bog, his hand squeezing the color from my skin.

I screamed and clung to Anne. He was no longer human at all, but the reptile I had seen in my nightmare. His white hair was now green scum, covering a naked gray head. The bones of his face were flattened and his eyes were pushed far apart to the opposite sides of his skull. Only the slits of his nostrils remained. Most of his face was a huge jaw, which cracked at the joint as he snapped at my calf with fanged teeth. I kicked my leg out wildly and the clawed hand scrabbled to keep its grip.

I was still holding my bow and I lashed out, beating the humped gray shoulders. Rosin puffed out from the strings in a gold-flecked cloud. With a howl, Bog released my leg. He turned about, twisting and writhing in pain, trying in vain to brush the rosin from his back. The rosin smoked and burned pinprick holes into his slick skin. The holes expanded into scorching teardrops, eating away the skin. I rapped him again with the bow and the rosin dusted his face. He raised his clawed hands to his eyes and shrieked.

He staggered away, lurching back and forth until finally he fell against the window. His eyes were gone, the narrow sockets bare except for thin white layers of skin that were peeling away like curling birch bark. The black wasp tapped her wings against the glass and Bog raised his head, quieting his moans to hear the sound. His searching fingers moved higher and he found the broken pane. He pushed his hand through the hole, his arm reaching outside. Then in a rush of water his body followed, his skeleton disintegrating as the gray sheath of wet skin turned into green fog and poured through the hole in the glass.

I stared at the pane, dirty droplets of rain sliding down its smooth surface. Beyond the window I could see the fading light broken by the trees as Bog escaped.

Anne was crying, holding me, hugging me where I lay across her lap. I glanced up, awed at the blazing corona of sun-bright hair and the molten tears that streamed down her burnished cheeks.

"It's all right, Cassie. It's all right," she crooned.

I nodded, too weak to answer. And then I started to shiver, my skin cold and streaked with mud and swamp slime. Anne released me just long enough to strip the wet clothes from my body. My teeth were chattering by the time she had wrapped the blankets around my naked body. The wool was rough against my skin.

Anne lay down beside me, settling my head in the crook of her shoulder as she had done when I was small. She smoothed back my hair at the temples and sang softly to me. It took some time. But the terror of Bog's attack faded, and I was comforted by the warmth of her arms, the lavender scent on her skin, and the soft, soothing melody. I didn't understand the words, if there were words at all. But there was no mistaking the longing in my mother's voice as she sang her version of the fiddler's sad waltz. *She knows him*, I thought as I drifted into sleep.

✦ chapter eleven ✦

I WOKE TO THE SUNLIGHT bursting through the uncurtained window and the sounds of a pickup truck gunning its way to our farm. I sat up and looked around, dazed, as the memories of last night returned. I was naked beneath the blankets, but my clothes lay in a neatly folded pile beside me. My violin and bow were stowed in the open case, the cake of rosin resting on the window ledge, sunlight pouring through it. There were no black mushrooms along the window frames, no brown water stains on the wallpaper. The room was as dry as it had been yesterday. I shook my head, the memories of last night too vivid to ignore. Then I ran my fingers through my hair and pulled out long strands of marsh grass. Not a dream.

The truck motor whined as the driver downshifted. I roused myself and peered out the window, the blankets wrapped around me. For a moment I was scared that I would see Melvin's battered black truck. But it was a cherry-red truck that appeared through the trees, coming to a grinding halt in front of the trash pile. A man got out of the cab slowly and stood before the garbage.

"Who is it?" Anne called from the studio.

"Father Tom's brother-in-law, I think," I called back.

"Come for the garbage." I watched him push back his billed cap and scratch his head in amazement. "Poor guy," I muttered. There must be a whole lot more there than he thought.

I dressed awkwardly, my clothes feeling stiff as laundry hung out to dry. Everything felt strangely normal when it shouldn't have been. Things had happened last night. Hadn't they? I touched the broken pane of glass in the window, ran my hand over the dry wallpaper.

Anne met me at the parlor. She had on Gunnar's black sweater, and her skin was pasty in the morning light. "Look, I don't think we should be cheap about this. Let's offer him some decent money to haul this stuff. Did you bring any cash with you?"

As Anne was talking, I felt even more confused and uncertain. I studied her face for a sign that she had been there when Bog dragged me under the water. That she had rescued me, that her golden arms had pulled me out of the depths of a swamp that had been here in this room.

"Cassie, are you hearing me?" she asked peevishly.

"Yeah," I answered, flustered. "I think I brought about forty bucks in my coat pocket. Take it."

"Go out and ask him in for some coffee, would you?"

"Sure." With her shoulders hunched and her arms crossed beneath her breasts, she looked breakable.

It was chilly, so I put on my sweatshirt and went out the front door, skirting the dried blood. If only *that* had been a dream, I thought miserably.

"Hi," I called. "Did Father Tom call you?"

"Yeah, he did, yesterday. I'm Rob Caldwell." He offered me his hand.

"Cassie Brittman," I said. It was a strong handshake, palm to palm.

Rob was pleasant looking, his fair skin newly sun-burned from working in the fields. He took off his cap, ran a hand through his reddish hair, and resettled the cap. He shoved his hands in his pockets and rocked back on his heels as he surveyed the pile. "Father Tom said you had some garbage that needed hauling to the dump."

"It's a lot, isn't it?" I offered, sticking my own hands in my pockets. I was hoping he still wanted the job.

"Yeah, pretty impressive. Did all of this come out of that little house?" he asked incredulously.

"Yeah, and there's still more to come. But I'm pretty sure my mom's friend can give you a hand."

He whistled. "Well, I can see it's gonna take a bit more time than I thought."

"My mom says to come inside first. Have some coffee with us and talk it over."

Rob scratched the back of his head and smiled at me. "Don't mind if I do. Thanks."

He followed me up to the house, hands still in his pockets, head tilted down. At the porch he frowned at the dried blood on the stairs and the front door. "What happened here?"

"Someone left a dead animal nailed to the front door."

"Jesus," he swore, looking worried. "Any idea who?"

I shook my head. Anything I said would be weird, or I'd sound like Poppie if I tried to explain. "Someone who doesn't like us, I guess."

We walked through the house to the kitchen and I introduced Rob to Anne and Gunnar. I told Gunnar that I had offered his help, and got teased about volunteering his labor without first asking. Anne and Rob haggled a little on the price, then worked it out. I lost all my money in the deal. Gunnar insisted that Anne take an extra twenty from him, and this time she did, even though she blushed as he handed her the money. The deal done, she poured out coffee and handed Rob a plate of hot biscuits.

"Wow, these are great," he said appreciatively, crumbs at the corners of his mouth. "You make 'em?" he asked Anne. Anne grinned and shook her head, pointing to Gunnar. His eyes opened a little wider in surprise.

I took one and split it open, slathering on the butter. Gunnar had bought some local wildflower honey and I dripped on a spoonful.

"How well do you know this Melvin Steiger guy?" Anne asked Rob.

He took a quick sip of coffee to wash down his biscuit and shook his head. "Not too well. No one really does, though he seems to be everywhere around here."

"When did he come? I don't remember a Steiger family from the old days."

"He showed up 'bout two, maybe three years ago. Bought the Pienkowskis' farm just over the swamp. But it hasn't done much but lie fallow." Rob took another biscuit and chewed it thoughtfully for a moment. "I had heard Melvin was interested in owning this farm. Some said he'd worked out a deal with your father."

"No. Neither of us would ever sell it to him," Anne said firmly. "Not him, or his whole clan."

Gunnar offered Rob a cigarette and he took it. Anne poured more coffee, then offered me some. I nodded, licking the honey off my sticky fingers.

"This here is a pretty farm," Rob said, blowing out smoke. "I grew up just over the way there, about five miles down the road."

"Is your family still farming?" Anne asked.

"No," Rob answered with a tight shake of his head. "I'd like to, but we just had too much bad luck and too many debts. Our herd got hit by parasites a couple years back and most of them died. We couldn't get the money together out of the crops to rebuild the herd. There isn't a farm around here that hasn't been hit with something in the last few years. My dad sold our farm and I've been doing work when I can get it in Ashland. But I miss it. Yes, I do," he added. I could see him measure us as city folk. Even Anne, who had been raised here, wasn't exactly farming material. "You know, your farm has some nice pastureland and a couple of good fields. Ever think of turning it into a working farm?"

"I wouldn't know where to start," Anne said with a smile, but I could see an inspired look cross her face.

"Well, best we should have at that pile," Rob said,

stubbing out his cigarette in an old soup can. He grabbed one more biscuit. "These are good, man, I got to hand it to you."

"Thanks," said Gunnar, brushing some extra flour off his jeans.

"We'll help, too," Anne said, quickly rising from her chair.

"Can I stay?" I asked. "I'm really . . . beat. I didn't sleep well at all last night. Maybe I'm coming down with something. I'd really just like to rest."

Anne stared at me and chewed her lip. "All right. It won't be for very long. But stay in the garden. You should be all right in there."

Gunnar followed Rob out of the kitchen, but I grabbed Anne by the elbow and held her back.

"What about last night?" I asked.

Her face went blank. "What about it?"

"You were with me. In the parlor," I started, fumbling for the words.

"I slept in the studio with Gunnar."

"But you came in and pulled me away from Bog. Didn't you?"

She was silent, her brow knitted on her smooth forehead.

"Didn't you?" I insisted.

"Later, Cassie. We'll talk about this when I get back. Just keep your eyes open and your wits about you. The winter hare is never far away, so I know you're safe here."

"What does that mean?"

Anne stroked my cheek. "Stories, old stories mingled with truth. I promise, when I come back we'll talk."

I let her go then. My ankle itched, and I reached down to scratch it. Pushing back my sock, I saw a ring of bruised flesh, a purple shadow circling the bone where Bog had grabbed me. *So*, I thought numbly, *it was no dream. Any of it.*

My whole life I had felt the strangeness of the farm, accepted it, but never understood it. My mother's silent fear spun into stories, Poppie's riddles painted into landscapes. The tension that was always there along with the beauty. Nothing added up ever. There was so much I needed to know—not just about the farm but about all of us. They had kept things from me. I saw the brown leather binding of Hannah's journal sitting on the kitchen hutch, and it occurred to me that perhaps Hannah could tell me what the others wouldn't.

I retrieved the journal from the shelf and poured myself another cup of coffee. Outside, I could hear Gunnar and Rob talking as they loaded garbage into the flatbed, followed by the trill of Anne's laughter. I took a sip of coffee and started reading.

It wasn't long before I stopped hearing them outside and became lost in the events of Hannah's life. It was easy to see that she had been smart and sensitive, and her daily entries carefully recorded all the little details, her thoughts and her private worries. It was as though I was there beside her.

The more I read and got to know her better, the

more I liked her. Her life hadn't been easy, even from the start. Orville, it turned out, was not the man she wanted to marry, but the one her papa insisted was the right choice. She had misgivings about him and she definitely didn't want to be a farmer's wife. She wanted to go to school and study medicine, even though it wasn't exactly allowed for women. But she followed her father's wishes and married the guy, packing away her medical texts in trunks, along with her dreams of school. They had a dairy farm for a while and then Orville got caught up in the fever over land speculation. He sold everything for a farm up north in Ashland. Hannah wrote about traveling north on the "scoot," the little train, and how uncomfortable it was as she bounced and banged her rear end on its hard wooden seats. But the land was beautiful, and after the flat prairies of the south, she was taken by the different shades of green in the pine forests and the sudden burst of blue lakes and white birch.

Life on the new farm was rich in work and poor in fun. Orville worked to clear his land of the old stumps left by the logging companies. He cut out the remaining timber to sell to the local mill, which produced shingles. Hannah had definite opinions about the way that Orville farmed. She had read a lot of articles in agriculture journals and seed catalogs. Orville didn't pay much attention to her ideas. She wanted to grow a variety of crops, potatoes, peas, and barley, to tide them over until the dairy herd was built up. But Orville insisted on planting wheat. Wheat was a man's crop, a crop that made money. At least for the first two years, anyway. Hannah was ready to concede that she had been wrong. But in the third year the soil gave out, and the crop suffered. In the same year, the price of wheat collapsed. Two prize cows wandered out into the bog and disappeared. Hannah wrote that on summer nights, she was sure she could hear them lowing somewhere deep in the tamarack swamp. It scared her and frustrated the hell out of Orville.

In those three years, she had remained childless. There were pages with nothing more than short bitter sentences that marked the beginning of her period. It was clear that she was more than a little anxious as Orville got angry with a land that wouldn't grow, cows that disappeared, and a wife who couldn't birth sons. Hannah noted that Orville had no intention of taking any responsibility for their childlessness.

As a side income, Orville had tried to keep bees. But the second year they had them, the hive swarmed and disappeared into the woods.

"Cassie? Cassie?" Anne called from the front door.

"Yeah," I answered, not looking up from the journal.

"We're going to the dump with Rob. We'll be back in an hour or so. We'll talk then. If you go outside, stay in the garden."

"Yeah, no problem," I shouted back. I waited until I heard the doors slam and the truck roar to life. The shocks squeaked and groaned with the weight of the garbage as they drove down the road. Then I returned to my reading.

JUNE 13, 1918. *Orville wants to hire a bee hunter to find our runaway swarm. The bee hunter searches the forest until he can locate the hidden site of our hive. It takes a man well versed in the secret signs of the forest to find a hidden hive. He must know where to look among the trees, the fallen deadwood, and even the underbrush. When he does find the hive's new nest, he marks it and then waits until the first frost. Then he smokes out the bees and harvests the honey from the wild hive.*

Orville has cut marsh grass and the little bit of hay we were able to grow in this wet spring. He was in a hurry to store it and now I fear we may yet be in trouble. Last year a barn burned down because of green hay heating up and then bursting into flame. Orville tells me I worry needlessly, but I cannot but help think it is his shortsightedness that has brought our farm to its present desperate state.

The seeds I ordered from the Northern Seed Co. arrived in time to be planted. I've marked off a big rectangle in the back of the house where the light is best. I shall have hollyhocks, bachelor buttons, nasturtiums, and cosmos. Katie Knaack gave me some peony slips, a clump of delphiniums, and lupines. But it's not all frivolous, for I have kept a place for joe-pye, boneset, and comfrey to ease our illnesses, as well as a place for a few vegetables.

I looked up from the journal, glanced out the kitchen window, and thought about Hannah's first garden. A rectangle of ordinary flowers and vegetables. It had been a tamed thing once, not like the wild, circular garden there now. I took the last biscuit off the plate and ate it as I continued reading.

> JUNE 20, 1918. *The Northern Seed Company held a barn dance last night in Ashland. Oh, I had nearly forgotten what a joy it was to hear music and dance. To see men and women happy to be together. Even Orville stopped being disagreeable and partnered me in a few of the contra squares. The dust from that old wood floor was terrible, though, and we needed a drink of punch to wet our parched throats afterward. The success of the dance was surely due to the fiddler. I had not met him before but he has a powerful arm and kept his bow on the strings almost all night without stopping. Orville has learned that the fiddler is also a respected bee hunter. He means to hire him out to find our swarm. I am pleased, for there was something in those eyes and in the way the music soared in my heart to make me think the fiddler is a spiritual man. Looking at his face, I cannot tell how old he might be, for he is distinguished by gray hair, but his eyes seem much more youthful. They twinkle like a boy's.*

I was startled seeing those words that Hannah had written so many years ago. I thought of Hannah at the dance, hearing the fiddle and, like me, being swept up in the music. It had to be the same man, my fiddler, Anne's fiddler, and Poppie's fiddler. He kept showing up everywhere.

AUGUST 31, 1918. *The fiddler has been on our land all summer hunting our bees. He came yesterday to tell me that he has found them and to show me where they had got themselves. Orville was in Ashland but I thought it no harm to follow him into the woods.*

How eerie the woods look when the light breaks through the branches and gifts the gloomy places with shafts of gold. The fiddler showed me many plants I had not known existed: stoneroot, good for kidney disorders, and sweet coltsfoot blooming near the marsh. There are even some in the swamps that live on insects, catching them in petals sticky with sap. The tamaracks are just beginning to change, sensing the cold nights and the shortening days. They have lost their green cast and are starting to fade to yellow. The farm and Orville seemed so far away the deeper into the woods we traveled. It was there that the fiddler asked me a strange question.

"What does your heart desire most? I will give it you in repayment for walking with me here and now."

What could I say to that? That this man might give me what my husband had not? I was a married woman, the ring tight on my finger. I answered nothing but in my heart, the old ache rose. A child, *I said to myself.* Grant me a child. *But outwardly I shook my head and answered that I was well content.*

The rest of the day was pleasantly spent and I think the light in the woods glowed a sweeter green than I had ever seen before.

I flipped the pages over slowly as Hannah went on about the fall: Orville harvesting the disappointing wheat crop, Hannah canning vegetables, salting meat, drying fruit leathers, and storing her carrots, potatoes, and turnips from her garden in crocks filled with sand. I turned another page and frowned at the rushed, sloppy handwriting. Ink blotted the margins and letters were smeared as if her hand had swept over the page while she scribbled her entry.

NOVEMBER 1918. *Pray God that I am not damned to hell for all eternity. Pray God that he will forgive me for my sin. But how could I have known? How could such a thing happen to me except that it was the Devil himself who taunted me and I in my weakness did not see it? Last month Orville left the farm to see a man in Ashland about hauling out more timber for sale. I was alone in the house as I often am, waiting for his return. I busied myself with chores until evening. An early and deep snowfall settled over the farm and the roads that night. Thinking I'd not see Orville again until morning because of the snow, I went to bed.*

My face burns with shame as I think of it. There came in the night a man in the very likeness of Orville. A man drenching wet with the fallen snow. I could not see him clearly, but when he laid his body close to mine, it seemed like that of my husband. How could I have thought otherwise? Except that when I think well on it, I must say that I knew it was not my husband. His manner was different from that of Orville. There was a gentleness in his touch that surprised me. And there was about him the sweet scent of honey and grass. God will despise me for it, but I found pleasure in our joining.

When I woke in the morning, the man I thought was my husband was gone. I spent the day in the parlor, just watching the pine shadows chase across the snow-crusted fields. Orville arrived late in the afternoon only to tell me that he had remained in Ashland for the night, being trapped by the snow. I said nothing, but the truth chilled me to the marrow.

My pulse raced as my eyes swept over the words. The fiddler again. He had done something to make Hannah believe he was Orville. And he had slept with her.

I could guess at the rest of Hannah's story and the beginnings of my grandfather's life. I turned the pages rapidly, my eyes scanning for the words I knew would be there. I stopped, seeing the phrase "with child at last" written all by itself on a page. Impatient, I flipped forward nine months. There, in a calm hand, Hannah had recorded Daniel Brittman's birth as though it were nothing less than a miracle.

I sat back, awestruck. The family secret was out, even if I wasn't sure what exactly it meant. The fiddler had known Hannah's hidden desire, though she had not spoken it aloud. And he had come to her disguised as Orville and fathered her only child, Daniel. The fiddler was my great-grandfather, though he looked not much older than Anne.

The character of Hannah's entries begin to change after Daniel's birth. Her elegant handwriting became a hurried scrawl. There were fewer entries and the passages became shortened, the words blunt. The barn had burned down, as she had feared, as a result of storing green hay. The winter had been too wet and the winter wheat had rotted in the field. But lady's slippers bloomed in the woods and the blueberries were plentiful. The bees returned to the hive.

Nowhere in her journal did Hannah write about Orville leaving her. It was almost as if, after Daniel's birth, Orville scarcely mattered. If she felt any shame in the matter of her pregnancy, she never mentioned it again. I also noticed that she had stopped recording dates, as if calendar time had ceased to be important. Only Daniel and the garden mattered to her. She talked about his first tooth on the same page where she drew up a list of wildflowers' names and their healing properties. "Milkweed or swallow-wort—raw root good for coughs and colds. Staghorn sumac—tea from roots to check bleeding." Every page had a new list as she gathered seeds, cuttings, and more knowledge.

In between the lists of plants, she kept records of the people she had treated, what had worked and what hadn't when it came to curing their illnesses. It didn't seem to matter to her that her neighbors thought she was crazy. She even joked about it once. "They say I'm touched in the head, but they come here all the same for my touch because they know it will cure them." The farmers' wives may not have invited her to tea or to their socials, but they trusted her with their lives, counting on her to get them through their pregnancies and look after their families. She had the healer's gift, and even if she seemed odd to them, they sought her out and paid for her services. I smiled, thinking that Hannah had found a way to practice medicine after all.

I closed the book and laid my hands on the worn leather. It explained a lot about Hannah's life and the spiral garden with its wild beauty. But it wasn't enough to explain the fiddler, or my grandfather. Had he grown up like her, "touched," or had he changed? He had left for France, married there, and then something had called him back. As Anne said herself, it was hard to leave the farm for good. Something always called them home.

I got up from the table, went into the studio, and found his sketchbooks. In the kitchen, I laid them down beside Hannah's journal, slipped off the ribbon, and opened the first one.

The drawings were boring. Sketches of France, guys in berets drinking wine at café tables, a stilted drawing of Henriette, a bowl of fruit. There was nothing here of the artist I knew. I closed the sketchbook and tried another, dated after his return from France.

On the first page was a sketch of a woman, her face distorted into leaves, her hands holding a sprig of heartsease. She stood in the garden, the long robes parted to reveal the curves of her nude body. The delicate pencil lines wavered on the page as though they were held by the grace of a spell. I could breathe on the images and they would scatter like ashes. Coming back from France, Poppie *had* changed. Something had grabbed hold of him, just like Hannah.

I turned another page and there was the fiddler, his unique violin resting across his knees, the keen eyes gazing back at the viewer. In the four corners Poppie had drawn leaping hares, their long ears flattened over their backs. That was it, I decided—another key fitting into the family lock. It was the wild magic of the fiddler that had called Poppie back. Maybe he went to France because he feared it and the madness that came with it. The young Daniel must have felt like Anne, alone and isolated by a brilliant but crazy parent. But he had returned home and, like Hannah, accepted the farm's gifts and made his peace with it. Anne was still struggling to stay away. I stared at the drawing for a long time, both afraid and intrigued. The fiddler was one part of our family history. But what was Bog? And what did Anne mean the night before when she shouted to him, *Not her, too!*

A truck revved angrily up the dirt road and, dimly, it occurred to me that Rob, Gunnar, and Anne had returned awfully quickly from the dump. The truck ground to a halt, the brakes screeching. A door opened, then slammed shut.

My ears strained to hear the sound of a second door and familiar voices. But it was quiet. Even the birdsong was stilled. I got up and hurried down the hallway just as the heavy thump of footsteps sounded on the back porch. I lurched to a halt. The doorknob jiggled and then twisted. As the door was forcefully wrenched open, I darted into the parlor.

✦ chapter twelve ✦

I GLANCED OUT THE WINDOW and saw Melvin's black pickup truck parked by the Saab. Bog had failed and now it was the troll's turn. The footsteps were loud in the hallway and I frantically looked around the parlor, cursing myself for getting trapped in a nearly empty room with nowhere to hide. Anne had said the house was protected. But it didn't seem that way now. I dove between the thick legs of the sideboard and the wall, trying to squeeze myself down into as small a knot as I could manage.

A foot kicked the parlor door open with such force that it slammed into the wall. I trembled in my corner, my back pressed against the wall. A hand covered with black fur curled around the doorjamb. The hand flexed and long claws appeared at the end of blunt fingers. In the hallway, someone snarled.

I was frozen with fear, though sweat beaded my forehead. Then, without warning, I was grabbed by the scruff of my sweatshirt and dragged upward. I felt a dull pressure against my chest and saw two brown hands, whorled like sculpted wood, clasping me under the arms. The hands hoisted me to my feet until I was standing, pressed hard against the wall. My knees wobbled.

Another hand, chalk white this time, reached out through the faded wallpaper and covered my mouth. I couldn't scream. I could barely breathe as I was ironed and flattened by the wooden hands, and pulled back through the brittle wallpaper.

I passed through the wallpaper's thin skin. The plaster cracked open like soft clay to allow me passage into the wall. The hand over my mouth kept the dry chalk and horsehair fibers from clogging my throat and nose. I could still see back into the parlor but as if looking through a dirty mirror. The hands continued to pull me backward into the yielding plaster until the old lath closed over my chest and thighs, hiding me within the wall. Plaster filled in the hole my body had made and the wallpaper repaired itself, knitting the tears, the white flowers smooth again on the gray background.

There was a soft muffled sound. Glancing sidelong, I saw the profile of a woman, her white face narrow and pointed. Her hair fanned out like spiderweb, weaving itself through the lath. She turned slightly to face me and her eyes gleamed. It was her hand that covered my mouth. The wooden hands belonged to a second creature, stunted and gnarled as an old tree branch.

"Shhh," the woody face whispered. It smiled and the corners of its mouth lifted sharply to just beneath the ears, shaped by twigs and leaves.

The walls are an illusion, Bog had said. So where was I now? I wondered.

Silenced by shock, I returned my gaze to the room

and saw Melvin Steiger standing in the middle of the now-vacant parlor, urinating on the floor. The stream of yellow urine left black, smoking lines of scorched wood in the planks. I knew it was Melvin because I had seen the truck and recognized the dirty coat he wore. But nothing else about him was the same.

His fat, ruddy face was gone, replaced by the flattened forehead and blunted muzzle of a wolverine. He lifted his head and sniffed the room. His black snout wrinkled as his lips curled back and he snarled, exposing yellow fangs. He stood vaguely like a man, but his shoulders were bunched forward like a dog about to drop and run on all fours. His chest was huge. Powerful arms swung at his side. His muddy boots were gone and the black talons of his feet rattled on the floorboards. He continued to sniff the air, knowing I was there and not there. His eyes glowed as red as the embers of the cookstove.

I wanted to faint. My head throbbed, my eyes itched, burning with the dust. My breathing was shallow because of the bands of lath pressed tight over my chest. The sweat on my forehead soaked into the dry plaster.

Melvin started to bay, the sound vibrating through the walls, shaking them until little bits of plaster crumbled around my ankles. A crack appeared in the opposite wall and a new panic seized me as I realized he meant to shake me from my hiding place. The hand over my mouth pressed tighter, drawing me farther into the dry flesh of the house. At my back I could feel a cool moist wind, as though part of me at least was outside.

Over the wall-cracking howls of Melvin Steiger, I heard the first few notes of a fiddle. My heart leaped. Melvin's howls quieted and his silver-tipped ears lifted, cocked and listening. He cringed, snarling as the fiddle's voice grew louder. The tune chased through the door and blew a gusting wind into the parlor that ruffled the stiff fur on Melvin's back. His ears flattened to his skull and he crouched lower.

The gray-haired fiddler appeared at the parlor door and his elbow jogged faster to free the tune from the strings. Growling and snapping his jaws, Melvin backed into a far corner.

"Shut up!" Melvin roared, and slashed the air with his claws as if to bat away the offending music.

But the fiddler, his green eyes cold as malachite stones, dug the bow deeper into the strings. The tune grew harsh, the double stops moaning with the coarse gait of the melody. He banged his heel into the floor, keeping time with the driving rhythm, and the dust rose into shallow clouds around his knees.

"Shut up!" Melvin shouted again, the sound of his voice more the man than the beast. "Enough, you son of a bitch," he bellowed. His face and body had changed with the tune. He had lost the wolverine's snout, his taloned hands, and much of his fur. But the red eyes of the beast still glinted with hatred from a man's face. "You've played enough."

The fiddler lifted his bow from the strings and slowly lowered the fiddle. "It's never enough for you," he answered.

"You've got no call to be here!" Melvin protested.

"On the contrary, son. I was invited while you were shut out. Your man failed and my folk have returned."

"Not for long. You think you've won, but you've lost. And soon, it'll be me that calls the tunes," Melvin snapped.

"It ain't over yet," the fiddler said quietly.

"Oh, but it is. Any idiot can see the blood's too thin. We plan on making short work of the ones that are left," he sneered.

"Go!" the fiddler commanded, and stamped his heel into the floor. Melvin flinched as the fiddler stamped again and the floorboards quaked. "Go. The red folk will not have the gate." His stare was wide-eyed and fierce, his knuckles white on the neck of his fiddle.

Melvin slouched along the edges of the room, avoiding coming too close to the fiddler. At the door of the parlor he snarled once, then disappeared down the hallway. Very distantly I heard the truck's engine whine, then roar away.

The white hand slipped off my mouth. I inhaled a mouthful of plaster dust and started coughing. The lath released me suddenly, and hacking noisily, I pitched forward. The wallpaper tore as I reappeared, spilling out of the wall's embrace. I lost my balance in the dizzying freedom of air and was only just able to grab the sideboard before falling on my knees. The fiddler reached out and caught my arm. He lifted me, holding me until I was steady on my feet again.

"It's all right," he said as I coughed up another mouthful of plaster. "Come into the kitchen. You could use something to drink."

My feet stumbled as he dragged me along. My throat was raw, and every breath I inhaled prickled my lungs. The fiddler sat me down at the kitchen table, placing his fiddle and bow carefully alongside Hannah's journal. He worked the pump until there was a bowl of clean water, then dipped in a cup and handed it to me. It tasted sweet after the chalk of the plaster. The fiddler took a blue bandanna from his pocket and dipped it in the bowl. I took the wet cloth and wiped my face. It was cool on my flushed, dry skin. When I looked at the bandanna again I saw dirt, cobwebs, white dust, and black mold.

"Gross." I shuddered at the mess in the handkerchief. I was afraid to touch my hair, which felt heavy with dirt and plaster.

The fiddler calmly took back his bandanna and rinsed it off in the water. The dirt swirled for a moment, then disappeared, leaving the water as clean as before. He gave me the rinsed bandanna and I washed for a second time.

"It could have been much worse," he said.

He sat opposite me and laid his beautiful white hands on the table. I regarded him warily as I sipped my water and tried to collect my scared wits. The fiddler had known about Bog, that's why he had given me the rosin. And he had saved me from Melvin. But for what purpose? I glanced at him over the rim of my cup. Though I'd not seen him do it, I knew he was one of them, a changeable creature like the badger man, Bog, and Melvin. But what did any of them want with our farm and us?

I put the cup down as the fiddler raised his eyebrows in a silent question.

"What?" I asked.

"You have the questions. I can see it. Maybe it's time to get this out in the open."

I nodded, wondering where to start. But as soon as I touched Hannah's journal, I knew.

"You tricked her, didn't you?"

"I gave her what she wanted."

"And Poppie, what did he wish for?" I asked.

"Guess," he answered, emerald eyes sparkling.

"His art. It got better after he came home," I answered, understanding the change in the sketchbook.

The fiddler nodded. "I gave him the choice. He could draw brilliantly, though no one else but him would see that, or he could make his work magical, a window into my world for others to see, though he himself would never be satisfied with it."

"He chose the second, didn't he, because at least it brought him success?"

"Oh, no," the fiddler answered, shaking his head. "He chose it for what he could give others, despite the fact that it caused him pain. A contented mind was something he willingly sacrificed, that others might see."

"Along with the rest of us. Anne and me," I muttered angrily. "So what was in it for you to offer such a bargain? Who are you, anyway?"

The fiddler folded his hands together, the fingers meeting like the folded wings of a dove. "Ah, you know me well enough. Just haven't caught on yet."

"Caught on to what?"

"Tell me, Cassie, how do you imagine the world?"

"Round," I said dryly.

"But filled with interlocking pieces, as in a puzzle. Take out too many pieces and the puzzle breaks apart, no longer held together as a whole."

"I don't see what this—"

He stopped me with one sharp glance and a raised hand. "You're one piece of a large puzzle. You can't begin to know how many other pieces depend on you for their survival as a whole. That's the problem with you humans. The day you discovered you had brains, you yanked yourself out of the puzzle, figuring you could stand on your own. While the rest of us cling to the pieces that threaten to break apart for good."

"I'm still lost," I complained. "If I'm an arrogant human, then what are you? Why was I able to go into the wall? Who was that woman behind the wall? And what do Melvin and Bog have to do with all this?"

"Patience," the fiddler snapped, clearly losing his. "We all belong to the world, your folk and mine. But we live within the forest, the water, the earth, and the rock. Once, long ago, we knew and respected each other. We were kin. But your folk put on airs and saw yourself as different from us. We were things out of nature that your folk wanted to control. So you shut us out, put yourselves above nature, and forced whatever remained of our mutual history into children's tales."

"You're fairies?" I asked, unable to hide my laughter. "The kind who drink milk on the back stoop?"

The fiddler slammed his fist on the table, his face reddening with anger. "Don't be a fool, girl. Or I may yet leave you to the fate Melvin and the Red Clan would have for you."

That threat quieted my laughter pretty quickly. I glared at the fiddler, not liking where this conversation was going at all.

"The Red Clan?"

"Yes," he said, "even among us there is division, for what nature seeks to create, nature can as easily destroy. The Green Clan has always held the way open for humans, but the Red Clan—"

"They're out for blood, right?"

He sighed and passed a hand through his hair. "Cassie, you've read Hannah's journal, I know."

I nodded.

"Then you know how the loggers came here and nearly wiped out these forests. They cut down spruce, white pine, yellow birch, and maple. They drained the bogs and swamps and planted wheat. They may come again in the future to mine copper and poison what is left of the land and the water. And all because they can't see into the puzzle, can't see that their fates might be linked to the health of these woods. These are my lands that are being laid to waste and my folk whose lives are being slowly destroyed. But yours may be next. For as we go, so do you."

"How can I believe you?" I asked, sobered by his words, but still uncertain. He had walked Hannah through the pines and who knows how he had pleaded his case before Daniel. Was he telling me something to get my sympathy? I still didn't know what he wanted from me.

The fiddler shook his head. "It's hard to see clear into my world anymore, to know my folk as they once walked the fields. But you have seen them, here in the garden. And your kind can feel the emptiness left by our absence. Something will remind you of it and a powerful grief will come stealing over you."

"The tune you played in the bar?" I asked.

"An old one. It's to remind your folk of what has been lost."

"All right, I think I get it. Sort of," I conceded carefully. "But why did you come to Hannah and then Poppie? What did you want from them? And what does Melvin want with me now?"

The fiddler picked up his fiddle and set the tailpiece against his armpit. He crossed his long legs, the elbow of his fiddle hand propped on his knee. He played a tune, the notes spilling softly into the room. And as he played he continued to speak.

"Our folk are much older than your human society. We have laws and rules, though they aren't the same as yours, and we honor them, mostly."

"Do they include letting Bog drown me, or Melvin Steiger chewing up our house and trying to kill Poppie?"

"Like your folk, he wants to live. He's not looking to cause sorrow and pain. He's looking to see that his Red Clan survives in a world made harsher by human greed and waste. Can you blame him?"

"And you? Where do you stand in all this?"

He grinned. "Wherever it suits me. For I also want to survive. But in a different way. Look here, this farm sits on the border between my folk, the last outpost of my world in these here parts, and your human world. These walls are an illusion; one step can take you into the green fields, the other—"

"Into the bogs. Yeah, I almost learned that last night."

"But if we work together, we can strengthen our two worlds, make the light shine both ways again."

"How?"

"Through a bond of blood," he answered simply.

I didn't like the sound of that.

"I offered Hannah a child. And that child became the bond of blood between my folk and yours. That gave me the right to rule here rather than Melvin."

"Poppie is . . . is one of your folk?" I asked, the thought spinning like a coin.

"Yes. He's of the Green Clan."

And then the coin dropped. "But that deal drove Hannah crazy. She didn't ask for that!"

"She wasn't crazy. She saw through the walls. She belonged to a larger world than the people around her. She was compassionate and she used what she learned from us to help folks around her, even though they were blind to our needs."

"The garden," I said.

"A place of power because of her," the fiddler added.

"And Poppie?"

"He, too, saw across the border and into our world. His blood made that possible. I bargained his human side into the contract by promising him that vision would find a way into his work."

"If the bond is there in Poppie, then why is Melvin here?" I asked.

The fiddler stopped playing. "If Daniel dies, there is no one left to honor the bond between my clan and yours. Without it, the border will close forever. I'm not the only one unwilling to let that happen. Unless I can make a new bond to hold the border open in my own way, Melvin and his clan have vowed they will take the contract in blood themselves. And it will be their right. If they succeed, they will earn the right to hunt any and take their lives as payment."

"Like rent?"

"Do you think Rob Caldwell and his family deserve to be rent?"

I shook my head, afraid of what Melvin's clan might do. The fiddler had not asked me yet what was my heart's desire. What would I ask in exchange to keep the border between us open? I didn't want to think about it because I knew he would know the moment it entered my mind.

"What happened with Anne?" I blurted out, trying to avoid my thoughts. "I know you must have tried. She recognized you in the diner, didn't she, and she was scared."

The fiddler humphed and scraped the bow over the bridge of his fiddle with an ugly scratching noise. I knew the feeling. Fighting with my mother did that to me.

"So what was it?" I asked, growing curious. "What did you offer her?"

"A mother," he said sullenly. "But she wouldn't strike the bargain and I came away empty-handed."

"A mother! Hah, did you get that one wrong." I laughed.

"I still don't understand why," the fiddler replied, baffled. "I heard the want in her heart as clearly as I heard it in Hannah's and Daniel's."

Well, I understood it perfectly. Anne could never have trusted anyone after Henriette dumped her, except me, the child and mother she created for herself. He should have offered her a lifetime of cookies.

"Cassie," the fiddler said, his gaze holding mine, "someone must accept the bond, or my folk will be lost forever. I will be lost. And if Anne will not, then you must."

"You're trying to trick me into it," I spluttered, leaning away from the intensity of those sharp green eyes. I loved Poppie. But oh, I didn't want his life. I would lose Joe, my friends, Anne, my chance to play music. I would be crazy and lost, just so these folk I knew nothing about could exist.

"No, Cassie, it doesn't have to be like that, I swear it. I can show you the way," the fiddler said. "I'm trying to keep us both alive. Without the bond renewed between my folk and yours, not only will you and Anne lose the farm, but I won't be able to protect you from Melvin and his clan taking the bond in blood. And because you carry the blood of my folk in your veins, there is nowhere you or Anne can hide. Will you do it, Cassie?"

The green eyes sparkled in the sunlight, held my gaze trapped. My face flushed, excited. The fiddler extended his hand to me across the table, across Hannah's journal.

"For the sake of the winter hare, the farm, your clan and mine. Will you make the bond with me, Cassie Brittman?"

✦ chapter thirteen ✦

THE FIDDLER'S WORDS MADE ME scared, and being scared made me angry.

"Why should I trust you? How do I know you're telling me the truth?"

"You know I'm right, Cassie. You've already seen into the border. The white deer in Hannah's garden, the small folk at your feet, and the badger who crossed your path as a true friend. And you also know how dangerous the Red Clan can be."

"Bog," I said softly. I would have drowned if not for Anne.

"Look with the eyes of my folk, given to you in Daniel's blood. Look with my eyes and know what will be lost here. Must Hannah's and Daniel's sacrifice be for nothing because of a lack of courage?"

I bristled, but the fiddler leaned forward and took my hand. "You can't tell me you don't feel a need for this place. But to keep it a price must be paid, whether it is dragged from your soul by Melvin or you freely pay the fiddler his due."

"That's what Poppie said in the hospital," I said slowly. "He said he had to pay the fiddler."

The fiddler released me and a spark glinted in his

eyes. His nostrils flared briefly. "A true son," he murmured. "I hadn't thought of that."

He stood quickly, scraping back his chair, picked up his fiddle and bow, and held them securely under his arm. "Perhaps there is another way. Daniel may yet pay the debt. But we must go to him."

"I'm supposed to wait for Anne and Gunnar to come back," I protested. "Anne promised to tell me what was going on. After all I've been through, I want to hear that."

"No. There isn't enough time."

"Enough time for what?" I demanded.

The phone rang and I jumped half out of my skin. I ran into the parlor and grabbed it before it had finished its third ring.

"Hello?" I panted into the receiver.

"Hello, is this someone from the Brittman family?" a woman's voice asked.

"Yes, this is his granddaughter. What is it?"

"I'm calling from the ICU at Ashland Memorial Hospital. We wanted to update you about Mr. Brittman's condition. He seems to be experiencing some new difficulties. His vital signs have dropped since this morning and we aren't sure we can bring the infection in his lungs back under control. We think you and your family should come to the hospital."

"All right," I said, my mouth suddenly dry. "All right. I'll get there as soon as I can."

I hung up the phone, my throat tight. The fiddler stood in the doorway. "That was the hospital."

"He's dying, isn't he?"

I nodded dumbly.

"Come on. We have to hurry now and get there before Melvin and the hunt come to know. Can you drive?"

"Um . . . sure," I said. I went to the kitchen and snatched Gunnar's car keys. I didn't have a driver's license and I'd only had a few lessons in the Toyota in an empty parking lot, Anne yelling at me either to give it more gas or slow down. But there was no other choice.

I scribbled a note to them, apologizing for leaving with Gunnar's car and told her call the hospital as soon as she could.

"Get your fiddle," the fiddler ordered.

"Why?" I asked, even as I bolted into the parlor to grab the long black case.

"You may yet need the rosin to protect you," he answered grimly. "The Red Clan don't take too well to it."

With my violin case dangling from one arm and the fiddler pulling at the other, we ran to the Saab. I flung myself into the driver's seat and jammed the key into the ignition. I was shaking so hard it wouldn't turn, no matter what I did.

"It won't start!" I shouted at the fiddler. "I can't turn the key."

The fiddler reached over, batted away my frantic hand, and calmly jiggled the key deeper into the chamber of the ignition. He turned it and the car coughed to life.

"Make it quick, but don't lose your wits, girl," he warned.

I took a deep breath and tried to settle my racing pulse. I needed to remember what Anne had told me about driving a stick shift, easing off the clutch pedal and stepping on the gas at the same time. I threw the car into first and we lurched forward, jerking like a rabbit until I got enough gas going in it. I clenched the steering wheel and tried not to look at the fiddler, who was clutching the dashboard.

"I'm just learning, damn it," I grumbled as I shifted the Saab into second and we jolted forward again.

"Then learn fast," the fiddler said, pointing down the road.

I saw Melvin at the entrance to the farm, and he was not alone. He was waiting in the middle of the road, his wolverine head shaking back and forth. He was flanked by a pack of shaggy, black hounds, their hackles lifted across their massive shoulders, staring us down with glowing red eyes. They had huge padded feet and claws that raked sparks over the asphalt. A horn sounded in the woods and they all began to bay.

"That there is the red hunt," the fiddler explained. "Whatever you do, don't slow down. Drive through them."

"I can't, there's too many of them," I cried as their numbers grew with every blast of the horn. They loped out of the woods and onto the road. And here and there between the trees I could see riders on horses that were so emaciated they looked like old hides stretched across skeletons. The riders' faces were hidden in the blood-red folds of their sweeping cloaks.

"Go!" the fiddler shouted, and jammed his foot over mine on the gas pedal. The car whined in the wrong gear and then shot forward as if hurtled from a cannon. I changed gears, to fourth and then fifth, as the car gathered speed. "Don't stop, just keep driving," the fiddler commanded.

I screamed when the Saab rammed into the body of the first hound. It smacked against the grille, went up into the air, and smashed into the windshield before rolling off the hood. I drove on, trying desperately to see through the cobwebbed pattern of cracked glass and smeared blood.

The road was a narrow gray ribbon edged in huge black hounds that bayed and leaped at the car. Their jaws snapped at the windows and I shuddered at the sickening *whump* of their bodies hitting the fenders. In the rearview mirror I could see the cloaked riders following close behind, their red, hooded capes billowing in the wind as they slapped their crops against the withered hides of their horses. Smoke issued from the horses' nostrils and coursed through their streaming manes.

A hard thud sounded on the roof of the Saab, and then another and another until it seemed as if we were being pelted by hail. Wizened faces appeared upside down at the windows amid a fluttering of leathery wings, and I realized the car was covered with bats. Bats with faces and clawed hands. They were long-snouted like shrews but with very human eyes and twisted mouths. They spit at me and swore as they beat their wings against the glass.

"Can't you do something?" I yelled at the fiddler. The Saab was swerving back and forth as I tried to see the road through the dense covering of flapping wings. One bat had pried open my window and had nearly succeeded in squeezing its furry body through the narrow opening.

The fiddler reached across me with the point of his bow and poked it hard in the belly. It squealed and lost its hold on the window, falling back into the snapping jaws of a hound. I released one hand from the steering wheel long enough to roll the window shut.

"Keep driving, and don't stop for anything!" In the cramped quarters of the front seat of the car, the fiddler began to play. From the fiddle came a high-pitched, eerie sound, the clear lilt of a woman's voice raised in song. I trembled at its purity. I glanced sidewise, awed, and saw that it was the carved face on the scroll that was singing, the wooden mouth shaping words in a language I didn't know as the fiddler ran the bow slowly over the strings.

At the first notes, the hounds edged away from the car, but kept pace with my increasing speed. The bats lifted away from the windshield with a terrified screeching. Farther ahead, I saw a mist forming between the pines. The slanting light of the afternoon sun changed color as the cool green of the woods bled into the gathering cloud of mist and spilled out on the road ahead of us.

The mist rolled upward into a high green wall, the golden edge of sunlight on the top like the breaking crest of a wave. I could just make out the silvery flanks of horses within the green, turbulent foam. The faces of their riders were eclipsed by a blaze of light. Hawks arrowed their bodies through the green mist, through the flocks of hovering bats.

The Saab plunged into the mist as if into the emerald water of an ancient pond. The riders separated to let the car pass, and I caught only the barest glimpse of their white faces, ruffed like owls or long like ferrets. A naked woman, her slender body a pale silvery rope over the neck of a wintry gray horse, brushed away the last of the clinging bats with a branch of pine needles.

I couldn't see the road but drove anyway, caught between the terror of slamming into an unseen tree and the blind faith that the green mist would not let me or the fiddler come to harm. All at once we burst through the other side of the green wall. The road was empty except for the bright sunlight. I cried out in relief and wonder. My thighs ached from holding my foot to the gas pedal and my fingers were stiff where they clung to the steering wheel. There was no one before me, and as I looked into the rearview mirror, there was nothing but the black road disappearing behind me. The red hunt was gone. So, too, was the green mist.

The fiddler set down his bow, his furrowed brow

damp with sweat. In the abrupt stillness, my memory tried to hold the last dying notes of the singing voice. I thought I would cry out of a long-lost sorrow. There was nothing I knew of to compare with its piercing beauty.

"Who were those guys who helped us?" I asked the fiddler, bewildered.

"Kin," he said. "The Green Clan—my folk and your heritage. They will keep the balance until the time has come."

We drove the rest of the way to the hospital unmolested. There might have been other noises, the gravel skipping away from the car, a horn, and the mechanical hum of the engine. I didn't hear them. I couldn't shake the sound of the fiddle's singing voice. Even when the fiddler told me to park beneath the shade of an old ash tree, he had to repeat it twice before I heard him clearly.

We got out of the car and the fiddler broke off a short leafing bough from the ash and handed it to me. Last year's berries dangled from it like little wizened jewels.

"The ash will protect you and Daniel," he said.

Holding the slender branch, I thought it seemed an unlikely weapon against Melvin's hounds. But I didn't argue with what I didn't know, and dutifully took it.

The fiddler grasped me by the shoulders, his strong fingers digging into my flesh.

"What bond will you make?" he demanded, his eyes blazing.

"I don't understand," I said, my voice faltering.

"My son is dying. And before I go to him I must know

what you will bargain if he is lost. Tell me now. Speak the words. Is it the fiddle? You have the gift for it."

"That gift is my own," I said angrily, lifting my chin. "I worked for it myself."

He nodded in agreement. "So you have." Then, more gently, he leaned close and the ash branch was crushed between us. "What is it, then?"

The words rushed out of me, unbidden. "I don't want Poppie to die now."

"There's more."

"I want him to know who I am again. I want him to look into my face and see me, talk to me. Not the god-damn trees, not the plants or anything else in your world. You took him from me. I want him back. I need him as much as you do." I pushed back against the fid-dler's hands, angry and hurt.

"Done," he said softly.

I stood there openmouthed and my anger became dread and doubt. I remembered how much their bonds had cost my great-grandmother and Poppie. "What have I done?" I moaned, and covered my face.

"The right thing, girl. And now to make it easier for us both . . . "

I raised my face from my hands and the fiddler gave me a sly smile. His eyes sparkled, like a boy up to mis-chief, as Hannah had written. He ran his long white hands over his face and transformed before my aston-ished eyes. Gone were the gray hair, the beard, and the pale pink skin. Gone entirely was a man's face and body.

Only the hard green eyes remained the same. It was my mother's face that stared back at me now with the fiddler's sly smile. Blonde hair draped the slim shoulders and I could even smell the lavender scent of her skin.

"What are you, really?" I asked.

"A familiar friend," he answered, using his own deep voice.

In spite of everything, I giggled. "You'd better let me do the talking."

"My fiddle," he said, Anne's face in a worried frown. "I must not be without it."

"Take mine out of its case and put yours in there. That way we can bring it into the hospital without attracting too much attention."

"Quick then," the fiddler urged, looking around and clearly hearing something I could not.

I silently apologized to my violin as I hastily turned it out onto the front seat and set the fiddler's instrument in its place. I put the rosin in my pocket and snapped the case closed. I went to sling the strap over my shoulder, but the fiddler stopped me.

"I'll take it."

"All right," I answered. "Just remember, don't talk. Tell me, is that how Melvin got in there? Is that how he fooled them all into thinking he was just an ordinary guy?"

"A glamour, nothing more," the fiddler answered. "Only you and Anne could not be so easily fooled."

We walked through the hospital, the fiddler silently

nodding Anne's head toward Nadine, who refused to acknowledge us. I waited for the elevator but the fiddler grabbed my sleeve and we headed up the stairs instead.

"Don't like those things," he muttered.

"Shh," I said as we opened the door and found ourselves in the lime-green halls of the ICU. We approached the desk cautiously. A nurse looked up from her paperwork and motioned the fiddler and me into a small private room. It must have been the staff's lunchroom, because in addition to the table and a few chairs, a neat row of bag lunches and filled Tupperware sat waiting on the counter. It was weird to be in such an ordinary room with the fiddler looking like my mother and the nurse rattling off terrible news in a soft voice. She explained that Poppie was dying, though she never used that word. Instead she talked about him as if he were broken pieces: his kidneys were failing, his heart wouldn't beat strongly enough, his lungs were filling up with fluid.

A tired young resident came into the room and continued to speak in a low, consoling voice, suggesting that we sign a "No Code" for Daniel. When his heart gave out, they would do nothing to resuscitate him and prolong his life artificially. I hardly heard them, my eyes on the fiddler as Anne's face stared anxiously at the dim light in Poppie's room.

"Yeah, okay," I said brusquely, wanting the talk of Poppie's death just to stop. "Later. We need to see him first, before anything gets decided."

The resident looked at Anne and silently she nodded her head and stood.

We entered Poppie's room, me holding the ash branch in one hand and Anne's hand in the other. At that moment I wanted the comfort of my mother's hand, even if it wasn't really hers.

Poppie lay on the bed, thin as a dried willow wand. His toes and feet curled inward, his hands lifeless on the sheets. His face was contorted by the tubes jammed in his mouth. His lips were blue. A nurse had brushed his gray hair off his forehead and his skin was waxy.

I felt as if the floor disappeared beneath my feet. I was falling, tumbling in the air, and there was nothing to stop me. "Oh, Poppie," I said, a fierce pain in my chest. I reached out to take his hand and stifled a cry at the coolness of the slender fingers.

"Give him the ash," the fiddler said. "And be quick about it."

Tears blinding my eyes, I placed the branch in Poppie's hand and closed his fingers around it. The black smudge of his writing callus was gone, peeled away in layers of drying skin. A weak sigh broke the rhythm of the respirator and I looked up in surprise. His shadowed eyelids opened with a painful slowness. The lips moved to speak around the respirator.

"We've little time. Hurry up!" the fiddler said urgently.

I turned, confused, from Poppie's strangely waking face and watched as the fiddler shook something out of

Anne's shirtsleeve. Two small men with faces like walnut hulls were complaining in raspy bumblebee voices. The fiddler continued to shake his sleeve and a third tumbled out with a soft thump onto the bed.

"Get up there, and don't be difficult," the fiddler ordered the three nutmen.

They scampered to the top of the metal railing and disappeared under the sheets.

"What are you doing?" I asked.

"Getting Daniel out of here," he said flatly.

"What!"

"Back to the farm, before it's too late."

"You can't move him now, they won't let us!" I exclaimed, and looked wildly toward the door, half expecting to see the nurse.

"Has to be done," he answered firmly. "They'll never know."

"And how's that going to happen?" I demanded.

"Look for yourself." Anne's mouth curved into a grin.

One of the nutmen had removed the respirator tube from Poppie's mouth and was wiping it off on the sheets. Winking at me, he started sucking and then blowing into it with gusto. Red digits in the ventilator machine were snapping on and off.

"Ease up. Too much and they'll be in here," the fiddler warned.

"Sucks to you," the nutman shot back, letting his body bloat up like a puffball mushroom on the forced air. The second nutman had succeeded in undoing the tangles of

IV needles and was busy squirting the contents of the bag over the wall.

Daniel lay like a corpse on the bed, his fingers still curled around the ash branch. The third nutman was grunting and swearing as he struggled to shove Daniel upright. He had huge hands that lay across Daniel's back like spades digging up an old taproot.

"Come on, old man, move, will ya?" The nutman looked at us with a sour face. "Are you morons, or can you give a feller a hand here?"

The fiddler reached out and pulled Daniel to a standing position. His spindly old man's legs shook at the knees, the flimsy hospital gown not long enough to cover his shrunken thighs.

"Poppie?" I whispered.

His gaze traveled over the room and then to the ash branch in his hand. A lock of gray hair fell forward. He smiled, and on his waxy face it was frightening.

"*Sorbus aucuparia*," he said hoarsely to the branch.

I backed away, not knowing what to make of this strange Lazarus who stood swaying on his feet. The nutmen had taken over the bed and were bouncing on the mattress while they manipulated the machines.

"Don't lose your nerve now, Cassie," the fiddler rasped.

"But what's keeping him alive?"

"The ash. And my blood that will bring his human body home to us."

"But how do we get him past the door?" I asked.

The fiddler tucked Anne's arm beneath Poppie's elbow. "Take the other side," he ordered.

"We can't just walk out of here," I said desperately.

"We can."

"They'll see us."

"They won't."

"But they'll know he's gone!"

Anne's eyes rolled as the fiddler's deep voice whispered harshly. "Stop arguing, Cassie. The boys back there know what to do. They'll leave a wooden changeling and buy us a bit of time."

"But all they have to do is come in here and they'll know it's not him."

"Not unless they can see into our world. And they can't. All they will see is the changeling, left in Daniel's place. So let's go."

"Home," Poppie croaked. "Home."

My heart was hammering and the sweat trickled down my back as the fiddler and I walked into the corridor, Poppie stumbling between us. In the glaring light of the corridor I couldn't imagine that anyone seeing us wouldn't stop us. We moved slowly down the corridor toward the elevator, and not a single nurse looked up from her desk. An orderly passed us without a second glance as she went collecting food trays. A scrub nurse gave us a weary smile as she headed for the nurses' station, a clipboard in hand.

"I don't believe this. Someone's going to find out," I whispered, hoisting Poppie higher.

"There's bigger things to worry about," the fiddler said tensely.

I stayed quiet then and put all my efforts into getting Poppie down the stairs, since the fiddler refused to take the elevator. Once we were in the parking lot, the wind belled Poppie's hospital gown, and he shivered violently with the cold. I wanted to give him my coat, but the fiddler said to wait until we got into the car, otherwise my coat would spoil the illusion. I nearly cried seeing Poppie's bony feet, the dried skin of his heels yellowed and cracked as he limped in pain.

We reached the Saab and I hurried to open the back door. The fiddler set my case down in the foot well and helped Poppie lie down in the back seat. Poppie drew his knees up toward his chest and I covered him with my coat as best I could. He was humming a broken tune and his eyes were shiny with a green glow.

"Home," Poppie said in his craggy voice.

The fiddler got into the passenger seat and turned back to Poppie. Anne's face dissolved and his own bearded one returned. "Hello, old son," he said quietly.

"I've come to pay the fiddler," Poppie answered.

"And it's an honor to receive you," the fiddler replied, then turned to me, his face drawn. "Get us back to the farm, Cassie, and be quick," he barked.

I didn't need to be asked twice, though it took a few tries to manage the clutch and the gas pedal smoothly.

"What will happen when we reach the farm?"

The fiddler paused before answering. "Daniel means

to spare you of your obligation. He will return to our world what is ours, and the blood of his human self will strengthen the border and keep the contract. The red hunt and Melvin's clan will no longer have a claim there."

"Are you saying he's agreeing to be killed?" I asked, alarmed.

"No, he's returning to us."

"But that means he will die, won't he? The human half, the half I know, will die, won't it?"

"It's dying already, Cassie. I can't stop that. This way, his death will have meaning, not only for him, but, in the years to come, for you and Anne."

"But you promised," I cried, hitting the steering wheel. "I made a bond with you and you cheated me!"

"I've done neither," the fiddler said harshly. "Not all of Daniel Brittman will die. And I will honor my part of the bargain with you when the time comes. Besides, it is his decision to choose the site of his own mortal death."

"And Hannah?" I demanded. "Did she choose hers?"

The fiddler ran his hands through his hair. "I lost her, it's true. One of Melvin's Red Clan came to her, a thing of light and seduction, hard to resist. She followed him to the swamps. He trapped her spirit and shifted the balance of power. It gave Melvin a bond, a right to cross the border into your world. Without Anne and without you I could not shield Daniel from Melvin's influence over the farm. He would have succeeded in killing him, had I not nudged Father Tom."

"Hannah met Bog? The one who came to me?" I asked.

"Yes."

"And the badger man?"

"One of mine," the fiddler answered.

Questions started to have answers now. "The hare on the street?"

"I needed to know if you could recognize one of your own kin," he said with a half smile.

"The knots in my hair?"

"The nutmen did it to protect you from Bog. He was looking for you, too, same as me."

"Did they sour the milk?"

"You left them no payment for their work." The fiddler shrugged, as if the answer were easy to guess.

"So when Anne left a bowl of milk on the stoop, the herbs in the windows—"

"They could protect her from the sleeping charm."

"That's why she came last night, but not the night before."

He nodded and I sighed, exhausted. It was like learning words in a foreign language, then gradually seeing them all come together into phrases and sentences. Though it made a kind of sense to me, it was still pretty strange.

"How was it you came to the farm today when Melvin was there, but couldn't come before?"

"Because Anne fought against Bog and won. It shifted the balance in my favor and allowed me to return."

"If Poppie pledges his human life to the green folk, what will happen to Melvin?"

"He'll lose the right to hunt here."

"Then if Poppie is so important, why isn't Melvin still after us?" I asked, nervously looking around.

"I don't know." The fiddler slouched in his seat, then straightened, suddenly tense. "Unless he seeks a different quarry."

Cold fear rippled through me. "Anne! She and Gunnar are probably at the farm by now and she doesn't know what's going on! But Melvin can't hurt her as long as Poppie is alive, can he?"

"Hurry," the fiddler ordered. "Before it's too late. The man you know is hardly alive and already the spark is fading."

I pressed my foot hard against the gas and the car shuddered as it responded. The twilight sky was a mixture of fading rose and orange over the tops of the pines. The trees sketched a black jagged line into the last of the sunset and night hovered on the horizon with a distant twinkle of stars. It would be dark by the time we reached the farm. I thought of the bats, the skeletal horses, and the riders in cloaks of blood red. And I thought of Melvin and his hounds chasing down my mother as though she were a wild hare. I jammed my foot on the gas pedal and leaned my body over the steering wheel, willing the car to go faster.

✦ chapter fourteen ✦

I DROVE RECKLESSLY, MY EYES trained on the darkening line of trees that hemmed the road. All I could think about was Anne—as long as Poppie was still alive, she might be safe—so that I nearly drove past the entrance to the farm road. I saw it in time to slam on the brakes and managed to turn the car onto the dirt road. The fiddler was bounced against the door in the wrenching turn. My violin slipped off the seat and down into the foot well. I could feel it resting between my foot and the gas pedal.

"Get it out of the way," I shouted to the fiddler.

He bent down to retrieve my violin, one hand braced against the dashboard. The car careened up the bumpy road. Through the trees, I could see the lights on in the farmhouse. I allowed myself a breath of hope that she was all right, that we had been wrong to think that Melvin would come here.

But as I turned the last corner, driving between a pair of scrub oaks, I saw Anne and Gunnar huddled on the ground near the house. They were trapped in a circle of light and surrounded by the baying hounds of the red hunt. Gunnar was bleeding from a gash in his head, and a screaming Anne held a kitchen knife, threatening the hounds that came too close. They darted into the circle, snapping at her feet and head as she slashed back at them with the knife. Melvin stood outside the rim of hounds and threw back his head, howling at the moon rising over the pines. On the porch I could just make out the faint outlines of a ghostly woman. She stood unmoving, watching. As Melvin howled, the shimmering light of her gown bled a rust color.

"Damn that bastard!" I shouted. "I thought you said he couldn't get her until Poppie was dead!"

"Not kill her, but he can hurt her and wear her down," the fiddler answered.

"We'll see who gets hurt here," I snarled.

I didn't think I would ever fall into one of Anne's panoramic rages. Years of being embarrassed by her had taught me to avoid them at all cost. But I was her daughter, and as I aimed the hood of the Saab toward Melvin's wolverine body, I let her example be my inspiration.

Melvin turned to confront my oncoming car. He lowered his head, his ears flattened to the sides of his skull. Caught in the glare of the headlights, his eyes gleamed bright red. He crouched, his thighs bunched to spring, and when the car was nearly on him, he jumped.

I saw his face for an instant. His body landed hard on the hood, shaking the whole car. One taloned hand swung wide and then smashed through the windshield in an explosion of glass pellets. I threw myself to one side over the gearshift, ducking as low as I could and crowding the fiddler. Melvin couldn't see me clearly through the rim of broken glass, but his claws scrabbled inside the car, shredding the roof and the upholstery trying to reach me.

I threw the shift in reverse, so that the Saab bucked and then shot backward, then grabbed the steering wheel, giving it a sharp twist, and the car swerved wildly and rammed into the trunk of a tree. The impact jolted Melvin loose. I heard him fall with a guttural yelp, crashing first into the tree and then through the bushes. I shifted the car back into first gear. The tires whined and groaned, but the fender was stuck fast, the metal wrapped around the tree trunk. The tires spun, chewing ruts into the mud.

"Take Daniel and head for the garden! You'll be safer there," the fiddler shouted.

Just beyond the mangled car door I could see Melvin's powerful body thrashing in the underbrush.

"How?" I cried.

"I'll give you a diversion!"

I climbed over the driver's seat and slid into the back. Poppie was sitting up, the ash held firmly between his two gnarled hands.

"Poppie, we have to go now," I said, one hand grasping his upper arm while the other hand found the door handle. "We have to hurry to the garden."

He nodded solemnly and gave me that eerie half-dead smile. "*Sorbus aucuparia*," he repeated.

"Ready," the fiddler cried, his gaze appraising the rising figure of Melvin Steiger.

"Yes," I answered.

"Go!" He grabbed the fiddle and bow on the front seat, threw open the car door, and leaped out. He ran, fiddle in hand, cutting across the long beam of the headlights and along the dark edge of the forest.

He was a streak of gray light, his body bent forward. The black hounds saw him dart past and abandoned Anne and Gunnar to give chase. I watched fearfully as I maneuvered Poppie out of the car. The fiddler changed, his shape growing long and low to the ground. And just before he disappeared into the shadows of the underbrush, I saw the long ears and the white flick of the hind legs of a hare.

As I freed Poppie from the car I looked and saw my violin case, still in the foot well of the back seat. My violin case, but his fiddle inside.

"Oh, no," I cried, "he's got the wrong violin!"

Melvin's snarl made me move fast. I snatched up my case and, clutching Poppie by the arm, stumbled toward Anne.

"To the garden," I shouted at her. "Go to the garden. We'll be safe there."

Anne saw me, her white face carved with terror. Gunnar moaned and his head rolled to one side. "Behind you!" she cried.

I whirled around in time to see Melvin running toward us, first on two legs, then dropping down to all fours. His lips were curled back over the snapping jaws. I backed up, dragging Poppie with me. There was no way we were going to reach the garden.

But Poppie held out the little switch of ash, though his arms shook with the effort. When Melvin saw the ash, the berries trembling, his body contracted as though hit. He turned away from the sight of the branch and his claws raked the earth. I suddenly remembered Anne's stories about the power ash possessed to fend off the darker spirits. I had no idea then how important that knowledge would be. The ash forced Melvin to retreat a little. But it didn't stop him entirely. He continued to stalk us slowly, prowling, his eyes averted from the sight of the green branch. Poppie and I continued to back up until we were near Anne and Gunnar.

I saw she was standing, and supporting Gunnar. His long arm was draped over her shoulder and she was bent beneath his sagging weight.

"Are you all right?" I asked quickly.

"Oh, God, Cassie, what does it want with us?" Anne cried.

"To kill us," I answered. "Can you walk with Gunnar?"

"I'll try. Poppie," she whimpered.

He turned to her, the ash firm in his hands. He gave her a distant smile. "Annie," he croaked, "I've come to pay the fiddler."

Melvin snarled and darted close enough to slash at my ankle.

I kicked out in surprise and his fangs dug into the rubber sole of my sneaker.

"Get off, you fat pig," I shouted, shaking my foot wildly.

Poppie lowered the ash until the berries touched Melvin's back. He let go of my shoe and withdrew, the air peppered with the stink of singed fur.

"You'll be mine again," he said in his guttural voice. "My hounds will take the winter hare, and it's either you or one of yours that will be my blood slave. The bond will serve the Red Clan."

"Stay close," I urged Anne, chilled by Melvin's threat. I held up Poppie's frail body on one side and hooked my other arm around Gunnar's side to help Anne. The violin case bumped against my hip.

The four of us moved backward like a huge wounded animal. Anne and I half carried, half dragged Gunnar and Poppie over the long grass, through the bushy path on the side of the house, and finally toward the back of the house, where Hannah's garden promised a refuge. Melvin stayed close, his jaws snapping at the air to remind us, his claws reaching out to slash an unprotected leg. Anne swore, Gunnar groaned, and Poppie wheezed like an old accordion as we moved, step by step, Melvin following us.

It seemed to take forever to find the flagstones at the edge of the garden. I cried out in relief as soon as my foot touched them. My legs quivered with fatigue, my arms ached from the strain of supporting Poppie and Gunnar. When Poppie's bare feet touched the flagstones, Melvin sat back on his haunches. Then he rose on two legs, becoming partially human again. Anne sobbed and Gunnar slid to the ground, too heavy for us to hold up anymore. I took Poppie by the hand and we stood waiting on the edge of the garden.

"How long do you think you can last?" Melvin said, his face taking on human shape. It wasn't much of an improvement.

"As long as we need to," I shouted defiantly.

Melvin gave an ugly laugh and spat. "He's nearly gone. You've lost."

Poppie was shivering, his body racked by thick coughs. The light in his eyes had dimmed.

Behind me I heard the wind rustle the leafy plants in the garden. Anne gave a soft cry. I turned. Out of the crackling dead leaves and tender sprigs of new growth, the fiddler's Green Clan emerged to stare at us with as much curiosity and wonder as we did them.

I saw now that it wasn't just Poppie's imagination that had created his drawings. They were portraits. The Green Clan's faces wavered between human features and elements of nature: a man wore a rough cap of braided twigs, and thorns were raised along the length of his arms. He carried a quiver of arrows slung across his back and a bow in his hand. Next to him was a girl, her long legs ending in bird talons and her eyes nearly hidden beneath a brow of feathers. Out of the snow-trillium patch rose tall columns of pale green light that condensed into women, their faces hidden behind leaves. At their feet were toads in black beetle armor, carrying spears. A flutter of wings caused me to look up as a barn owl drifted silently over Hannah's garden. The wings opened wide and a man appeared in the place of the owl. His face was framed by a feathered ruff and his eyes were perfectly round and golden. A sword hung at his waist from a thin vine of fox grapes.

The air was moist with the scent of earth. The wet piles of leaves parted to show a rank of tall mushrooms. Their white, speckled caps were pushed back and I saw faces beneath them, the creatures' naked bodies as they dug themselves out of the loosened soil. Their tiny hands carried baubles of light.

A woman swirled out of the stately yarrow stalks in the center of Hannah's garden. I marveled again at the luminous white skin, the soft rustle of her robes as she moved. She held the mask of leaves in her hands and I saw her face, round as a child's, her mouth small and her nose snubbed. Her hair was the feathery green leaves of the yarrow, the fronds spiked with frost.

Poppie turned to greet them, his haggard face softened with joy.

There was a distant baying, and Melvin's wolverine ears perked up at the sound. He threw back his head and roared with triumph.

"They have the winter hare!"

"Not if I can help it!" Frantically, I opened my violin case and pulled out the carved fiddle. Melvin snarled when he saw it, but his face showed contempt.

"You can't play it!" he scoffed.

"Watch me!"

"You don't have the skill!"

"Says you," I retorted, and tucked the instrument under my chin. It felt so different from my violin. The weight was heavy at the scroll, the balance point of the bow awkward. I hesitated, a sliver of doubt in my hands.

Melvin saw it. "You'll destroy them all," he taunted.

I closed my eyes, shutting out the sight of his face, and placed the bow across the fiddle. All I could think of was the fast and furious charge of the partitas. This was going to be my real recital, I thought grimly, standing here on the edge of this world and another, playing for our lives. I drew the bow down across the strings.

There was a horrible sound, the horsehair screeching like a cat being pushed under a door. The face on the scroll woke, the eyes glaring at me with outrage. The outer flagstones of the garden erupted out of their sockets and some were tossed high into the woods. The green folk drew back in mute horror at my miserable attempt. Anne covered her ears at the sound and Poppie crumpled to the ground.

"What the hell's happening?" I shouted. "I can play this!"

"Not on me, you can't," the woman on the scroll said.

"Then help me out! Tell me what to do!"

"Don't think," came the waspish reply, and I wondered to myself if all violin teachers—on my side of the world and theirs—were alike.

"What kind of help is that?"

"Your thoughts are sticking to the strings. Open your ear, your heart. What is there will follow," the woman said gently. "Try again."

I closed my eyes and tried not think, just to be open to the sound, to the stirrings of my heart.

I pulled the bow slowly and the sound was sweet but shaky. I trusted my fingers to find the notes, the bow to catch them on the strings, and the face of the scroll to sing them out. I listened and heard the voice of the fiddler's violin shape the world of the green folk. The notes fell on the neck not as places set between the finger and the string, but as tiny flecks of the green world: dust from the wings of a moth, gold pollen, the black spoors of a fern, and the teardrop nut shaken from the pinecones. I inhaled deeply, the air fragrant, and imagined the garden's spiral path, the stones tracing inward like the curve of a snail's shell, drawing me into the center of the green world. I opened my eyes and saw that the world around me had changed.

It had been night in the garden. Now it was day, the sun's rays brushing gold paint over the green mantle of the pines, which somehow looked taller and broader than I remembered. Hannah's garden stretched wide and round, the tall spikes of blooming flowers everywhere, color blending together in dappled shades of light and dark. Across a narrow plain of shifting bronze grass I saw the winter hare, its body pressed low against the ground as it slowly gained distance from the hunting hounds.

The gray-haired fiddler was the winter hare.

And suddenly I lost it, my bow arm hesitated as my fear for the fleeing hare caught me up short. The woman on the scroll stopped singing and all the violence and clamor of the night crashed over me. The light vanished, and the trees looked flat. Anne was sobbing loudly, the hounds were baying, and a pair of crows cawed harshly, swooping now and again into the underbrush. I heard the staccato snap of twigs and branches and the steady drumming of someone running hard. At once the hare broke free of the underbrush and with a burst of speed lit out over the long grass toward the garden, zigzagging, leaping, and twisting his body high into the air to escape the hounds. Melvin was standing on the edge of the garden, still dazed by the song of the fiddler's violin. The hare boldly jumped onto Melvin's shoulder, then, springing off the wolverine's sloped forehead, landed in the garden near my feet.

The hare tumbled head over heels and rolled into a patch of thistles. Out of the broken branches scampered confused and frightened creatures. Melvin shuddered to life and found himself surrounded by his own frenzied pack. He roared with fury, seeing the hare in the garden, and struck one of his own hounds dead with an angry slash of his talons.

The hare lifted his ears high into the air to mock them all and banged an indignant heel into the earth. Then he raised up on his haunches and out of the furred pelt stretched the long body of the fiddler. He snatched the fiddle from my hand, panting hard as he looked it over, caressing the back and neck.

"Poppie? Poppie," Anne sobbed, her hand resting on my grandfather's shoulder where he lay on the ground.

Poppie was curled into a tight knot, the ash crushed in his fingers. Only the faint wheeze of his breathing told me that he was still alive. His eyes were opened but unseeing, reflecting the moonlight. I touched him lightly and his body felt stiff.

The fiddler bent down his face close to Poppie's and sighed. He looked at me soberly.

"The time's come. Look, they've prepared the way for him."

Bells chimed and I turned at the achingly sweet sound. They were there, the white deer, waiting for him. They were still women in gowns of silken light, hemmed with the soft needled boughs of white pine. Their arms were covered with bark and around their necks were beads of amber. One woman proudly carried a rack of horns on her forehead, and another a crown of leaves made from the silvery branches of the aspen. The third had twisted sprigs of ash in her braids, the tiny berries dangling like rubies.

The green folk parted before the trio as they moved slowly around the curved path of the garden to where Daniel lay. Anne and I stepped back as they surrounded his rigid body. With effort, the fiddler raised my frail grandfather to his feet once more. Poppie's head lolled to his chest, his arms dangling weakly.

Around his wrists the horned woman tied a wreath of heartsease and harbinger-of-spring. They crowned his head with bittersweet and in his hands placed a flowering hawthorn branch to join the ash. They sang, their voices low and murmuring beneath the chime of the bells. And when they lifted his head I saw his face and knew that my grandfather had died.

The mortal man had dedicated both his life and, now, his death so that the doorway between our folk should stay open. And as the human half of him was taken as a gift into the green world, his other self emerged: a creature of shimmering light, with eyes of burning emerald, wearing a mask of oak leaves and ivory ram's horns curled around his temples. He looked at Anne and me, the two of us gripped by a terrible, wrenching sadness, and he opened his hands to us in a gesture of quiet surrender. Those, too, were not as I had known them. The long, white fingers once stained with ink were now delicate fiddlehead ferns that uncoiled into fronds of brown bracken.

"Come to me, Cassie," Poppie said, his voice as faint as the brush of bird wing. I moved toward the creature of light, of greening boughs and wet bracken, searching the mask for signs of the man I had known, even as I knew that man was lost to me forever. The coiled horns tilted down. He closed his arms around me, enfolding me in a green world where the air was damp and fragrant with the scent of pitch. His chest was made of the pines' soft boughs, and when I laid my head against it, still praying for the slow beat of his heart, I heard instead the rasp of crickets and the long sigh of trees on a summer's day.

"Don't leave me, Poppie," I managed.

"Never," he answered with the creak of old boughs. "I love you. Always have. You and Anne are to me as the fruit to the flower. And I have shed this old husk that the seeds of my hope and my joy should remain. Watch over the garden, Cassie. And in it you will always find me."

He released me, opening his arms wide, and I looked up to see his leafy face raised to the stars.

The bells chimed louder, piercing the night. Poppie turned and walked with measured steps over the flagstones, following the women. The fiddler followed, playing a hymn to the wildness, to the green world, and to the joyful homecoming of one of their own.

At the edge of the woods, the light rippled and changed like an aurora borealis. The green folk were all there, waiting for Poppie. The red folk were there, too. Bog rode a skeletal horse whose reins were twisted vines of mistletoe. He wore a coronet spiked with spears of red sumac and, around his eyes, a band of black cloth. Melvin marched at the head of his people, carrying a long-handled scythe, rat skulls dangling from the crooked blade. His pelt glistened in the wavering light. Beside him padded the hounds, their glowing red eyes like sparks of fire. A drum and the nasal whine of a reed horn marked their passage.

Somberly, and without a glance in our direction, the rest of the Red Clan turned their horses and followed on the heels of the Green Clan. *A truce*, I thought, *a rare moment of balance when the rules of honor were obeyed.*

We watched until the sound faded and the light scattered on the wind. Anne shivered in the cold night air and Gunnar moaned from where he lay on the ground.

"Come on," I said to Anne, my voice sounding thick as syrup. "We've got to help Gunnar."

"But how? He's badly hurt. He needs to be in a hospital. And the car . . ."

I turned and saw the mess I'd made of the Saab. "Maybe I can get Father Tom out here."

Anne shook her head. "They cut the phone lines. We're alone."

I looked desperately at the house, trying to think of what to do. And then I saw her. She came down the kitchen stairs, shy and ghostly, the outlines of her frame like dust in the moonlight. But as she neared, her features grew clearer, as if she took strength from the soil. Once in the garden, she smiled and wandered along the path, bending and stooping to collect a little bundle of plants. She pushed back the strands of black hair that had escaped a comb. Snails clung to the hem of her skirt, and around her waist she wore a belt of marsh marigolds.

And when she stood before me I smiled to see that she was small and dark like me.

"Hannah?" I asked.

She offered a smile in return.

"Are you free of Bog?"

She nodded again, sadly. She bent to Gunnar and stroked the hair back from his pale forehead. She laid a collection of plants on his chest. Finally, she cupped his face with her hands and forced her breath into his mouth.

She drew away from him, smiled with satisfaction, and stood once more.

"Cassie, look," Anne said.

Gunnar's wound had been stanched, the blood no longer flowing out of the gash. His breathing was slower, more regular. His body was relaxed. He had found relief from the pain.

Hannah was walking to the rim of her garden, heading for the woods. I scooped up the plants from Gunnar's chest and started after her.

"Please wait," I called.

She paused at the edge of the garden, but didn't turn.

"I don't know what to do with these," I said.

She turned her head slightly in my direction. "It's all there in the journal, child. You'll find the way."

I watched her go then, following the same path through the woods that the green folk and my grandfather had taken. Her form rippled, solid and then fractured among the pine boughs. She passed beneath the high feathery branches of a tamarack and disappeared into the dense brush of the swamp.

We were truly alone on the farm.

Anne and I carried Gunnar into the house, his weight nearly toppling the two of us. I raked up the coals in the cookstove and put a kettle of water on to boil. Using Hannah's journal and the plants she had left me, I made a poultice for Gunnar's wound.

"How much does he know?" I asked Anne as we covered him with blankets.

She shook her head. "He never saw the animal that attacked him. And I don't think he'll remember much after that."

"Maybe it's just as well," I said softly.

I made Anne get some sleep, and when she did I sat up and waited. I knew that someone would come looking for us when Poppie's nutmen scuttled out of the hospital. It was just at daybreak that I heard a car turn up our road.

I hurried to the porch. A priest in his black jacket and white collar was getting out of the car. He stared at the Saab wrapped around the tree trunk, its windshield shattered.

"Father Tom?" I called.

He turned quickly and I saw the relief on his face. "Cassie, is that you?"

"Yeah. Thanks for coming out here. We've had a helluva night."

"I've been trying to reach you since midnight. But I think your phone must be off the hook or something, because all I got was a busy signal."

I paused. "Poppie's dead, isn't he?"

"Yes, he is. I'm very sorry for your loss," he said with sympathy. "But it was peaceful, I can tell you that."

For a moment, I saw the vision of Daniel Brittman rising up like a tree in the center of the garden, the chimes ringing around him. "Yes," I answered, "I expect it was."

"But what happened out here? Is Anne all right?"

I had spent a good part of my time watching over Gunnar constructing a story. I told it now to Father Tom, surprised at how plausible it all sounded: When Anne and I had returned from the hospital, a bear had crossed our path and she had lost control of the car, smashing it into the tree. Gunnar, trying to help us, had been attacked by the wounded bear. The phone wasn't working, and so we had muddled as best we could through the night. But Gunnar needed to go to the hospital and soon. It didn't take us long to get Gunnar into Father Tom's car. As we drove back to Ashland, I wondered what the nutmen had left in place of Poppie's body.

✦ ✦ ✦

It was almost funny the way it all worked out. Deferential nurses let Anne and me enter the dimly lit room alone, and as we pulled back the screens, we nearly burst out laughing. There in the hospital bed was a rough-hewn wood sculpture of a man's body—a changeling, spelled to look like my deceased grandfather. Except the artist had gotten creative, and added a pair of rabbit ears.

"Think the fiddler did it?" I asked Anne under my breath.

"No. It looks like Poppie's work," Anne said with her first smile in days.

Before we left the room, we struggled to rearrange our expressions to show proper grief.

While the wooden corpse managed to fool the doctors and nurses, we didn't want to press our luck trying to get it past the morticians. We had the changeling cremated, placed the ashes in a cedar box, and had the funeral at Holy Trinity Church. A lot of people showed up—Poppie's agent, other artists, people just curious about the reclusive Daniel Brittman, and, of course, the six o'clock news. It was a circus really, but I didn't mind it. Father Tom said some words as they set Daniel's headstone next to Hannah's, but I was distracted by the glory of the day, filled with sun, the sharp scent of earth, and the green of new growth. A hawk circled lazily overhead.

I had managed to find my violin—the fiddler had stashed it beneath a blueberry bush during his flight—so I played "Amazing Grace." The sound was different. Or maybe it was my ear, changed since I had played the fiddler's violin.

Gunnar healed rapidly. It came as no surprise to learn that Hannah's poultice had made the difference in his recovery. We snuck him in hamburgers and a couple of beers after he got well enough to complain about the hospital food. Those visits were cheerful ones. Anne even began to chat with Nadine. But it wasn't until we were in a rental car heading home, when Gunnar was wreathed in the smoky haze of his first cigarette, that he actually gave us a decent smile.

As we headed back to Rose Bay, I felt an intense longing, a mixture of grief and joy. Poppie was dead and Poppie was alive, transformed into something magical. Nothing would ever be the same again.

✦ epilogue ✦

THE FIDDLER KEPT HIS PROMISE. Each time I went north to the farm, I felt my grandfather's presence as I worked in the garden or strolled through the pines. I could talk to him and feel his answer in the brush of the boughs. At the end, Poppie had said what my heart most needed to hear, and in a new way, he continued to say it.

Poppie's sacrifice bought us the farm, the time to enjoy the farm, to see its majesty, to feel our connection to the Green Clan without fear of madness. Maybe things would be different for Anne and me. Maybe we would be able to keep open the gate without losing ourselves in the bargain.

As Anne and I picked up the pieces of our student lives, I came to look on her with new eyes, too. Anne had refused the fiddler, she had fled the farm even though it pulled on her, because she loved me. Our life wasn't perfect, but I realized that I had never known a day when I couldn't talk to her. She had been courageous, fierce in battle and protective of those she loved. Old hurts were mended, and I weighed in with a new appreciation for my warrior-queen mother and—for the first time—her boyfriend.

Other doors opened in the most surprising ways. It

turned out that Poppie's agent had squirreled away all of his checks into mutual funds, and suddenly Anne and I had more money than we had ever known. With Anne's blessing, I bought a very expensive violin and a beautiful bow. With mine, she bought herself and Gunnar two plane tickets to Sweden and left for a summer break. I stayed home, spending most afternoons in the park studying about wild plants and gardening. I had an idea forming and I needed a bit of time to develop it. Joe taught me how to drive, and I traveled back and forth between our apartment in the city and the farm.

On one of those trips, I went to Rob Caldwell and asked him if he wanted to make a bargain. If he helped us restore the farmhouse, he could work the two fields and use the pasture, provided he did only certified organic gardening. He liked the idea as much as Anne had, when I'd first suggested it. I also called up a county agent and had her come out and look at Hannah's garden. She was blown away. Some of the plants had been on the endangered list for over a decade, a few listed as gone forever, and yet here they were, thriving. She joined me in the garden and helped me to learn more about these rare plants and their care. In return, I gave her small cuttings and seeds that she took to the nature conservatories and planted. Knowing the folk that dwelled within those plants, I hoped that in this way, the gate would open wider, and more of the world would be touched by the wonder of the Green Clan.

Ever since the night I played the fiddler's violin, I

haven't heard music quite the same. Beneath the calculated notation of composed music, there is always another voice leading me into the green world beyond my own. Something of that wildness and unrestrained joy has been joined permanently to the music I play on this side. And when I see the fiddler some Wednesday nights at the Dubliner, he raises his bow in salute.

That was my legacy and my heritage: I was the great-granddaughter of the winter hare come down from the moon to play the fiddle. I had the blood of the Green Clan in my veins.

✦ ✦ ✦

There was one thing more that I needed to do besides restoring Hannah's garden. I needed others—my friends, the people I loved—to see what I saw, and to experience the world beyond the border.

Just before school started, I invited Joe, Genie, and the redheaded fiddler—who had turned out to be an Italian transfer student named Carlo, as well as Genie's new boyfriend—to join me up at the farm. We worked together in the garden, and in the late afternoon, as we took a break to drink lemonade and eat sandwiches, I told them the whole story. All of it. Leaving nothing out.

"Have you been smoking something?" Genie asked me playfully.

"*Che fantastico*," Carlo muttered. "Do I understand you right?"

"It's all true," I said simply, and saw the boys look at each other. "Just wait, you'll see."

At dusk, I set out a bowl of milk on the back stoop. We held our instruments and waited quietly, perched on the top step. Genie giggled, but I could see she was hopeful, watching every twitch of the branches.

And just as the sun dipped below the jagged line of the trees, the green folk tumbled out into the cool shade of twilight. Frog-legged, feather-faced, caps of thistles, and trailing moth wings. Joe gripped my hand as the smallest of my folk scampered to the bowl to drink.

"Look there," I said as the lanky form of a man approached the garden cloaked in a faint evening mist. He held a fiddle beneath his chin and the rising moon poured its light over the long silvery ears that were laid down his back. He played the opening measures of a reel and the rosin sprayed from the bridge of the violin like pollen across the wind.

"Do you want to join them?" I asked my astonished friends.

I picked up my violin. Joe adjusted the strap of his mandolin over his shoulder and stood, clenching the pick between his teeth. Genie caught Carlo by the hand. Together we started walking out to meet the dancers in the grassy field. Joe plucked his mandolin strings, the tune crisp and clean in the cool evening. The fiddler hammered his heel into the ground, his bow dancing over the strings, and began a tune. The green folk crowded the field, dancing and tumbling over one another in the dew-drenched grass.

"Unbelievable," Genie shouted over the music, her

face shining brightly in the moonlight. A woman dressed in peeling birch bark twirled around her into the arms of a man dressed in a coat of skunkweed leaves.

I threw back my head to laugh and Joe was there, leaning down over his mandolin and planting a kiss on my mouth. "I always knew you were special, Cassie Brittman."

"Welcome to my family," I said.

I can't say how long we played and danced. But sometime late in the night, we all lay down, exhausted, in the grass, stared up at the stars, and listened to the fiddler play his sad waltz once more. It was different from that night in the Dubliner. I knew the tune now. I saw how out here in the open it made the stars tremble, the wind sigh through the branches of the old pines, and the grass smell sweeter. It was a melody that went deep into my heart, sadness and joy twisting like the twin strands of a single rope. As my eyes began to close, I could feel my grandfather's hand brush my forehead, and I imagined him among the green folk smiling at me and my friends.

We woke early, our instruments at our sides. I sat up and rubbed my face. The long grass swayed serenely, a few wild daisies waving a cheerful good morning. There were no signs of it having been trampled by dancing feet the night before. Joe woke and sat up beside me, a sleepy, amazed smile on his face, the blooming stalk of a trillium behind one ear. He leaned over and gave me a slow kiss.

"Look," he said as we parted. He pointed to the

expensive new violin lying across my lap. I picked it up and the laughter bubbled up in my chest.

The scroll had been carefully carved into the likeness of a hare, the two ears pointed straight up to catch the sound of an air-tossed tune. I tucked the instrument under my chin and found the weight and balance just right on my shoulder. The carved hare grinned at me from the scroll, and as I drew my bow across the strings, I discovered they were still in tune.

Midori Snyder

is the daughter of a French poet who taught contemporary African literature and an American ethnomusicologist who played in Japanese Gagaku ensembles and gamelan orchestras before finally settling on Tibetan popular opera. She grew up amid visiting scholars, poets, Indian and Tibetan musicians, African and French authors, and a small town's worth of graduate students and professors. She has lived in university towns across the United States, as well as in Africa and Europe.

She is the author of six acclaimed novels and many short stories as well as a mask-maker, a practictioner of Shotokan karate, a classical (and Celtic) mandolin player, an M.A., and an English teacher. She and her husband, Stephen, have two teenage children.

Midori Snyder lives in Milwaukee, Wisconsin.

28 Days